Kiss OF

DEATH

A NOVEL BY

Chris Renee

Life Changing Books in conjunction with Power Play Media
Published by Life Changing Books
P.O. Box 423 Brandywine, MD 20613

Library of Congress Cataloging-in-Publication Data;

www.lifechangingbooks.net
13 Digit: 978-1934230466
10 Digit: 1934230464

Dedication

This book is dedicated to two women who have both profoundly enriched my life.

Ms. Denise Whitney, although I know if you were still here, this would not be a book that you'd read, but I still hope that you are proud of me. The spiritual guidance you have given over the years will never be forgotten. Thank you for loving me without judgment.

Deborah Lynn Jones when I wrote my first book and you asked me why I didn't dedicate it to you, I jokingly said, "Because you aren't dead". How I wish I never said those words from my mouth. Losing you is something that I don't think I will ever be able to get over but knowing you for 33 years is something that I will always cherish. Not too many people can say they had an aunt like you. You taught me how to always have pride in myself as a black woman and that is priceless. Until we meet again, Suga, all I can say is what you said every time we departed; "Peace, Love and Collard greens.

Acknowledgements

As always I have to first thank God for loving me in ways that can only be imagined. Thank You for knowing what's best for me even when I don't understand. I am forever grateful and humbled that You continue to love a sinner like me.

Much love to my family, friends, those who encourage me, those who hate me and even those who have yet to meet me. It is because of you all that I inspire to be greater than what I am. When my name finally hits that NY Times best-seller's list, we are going to jam one time!

To my LCB family, thank you for welcoming me in with open arms. This has been a crazy journey and I am glad that I broke it in with a team that is not only supportive but also amazing. Leslie, I have to really thank you for the Vampire nightlife that you work in. You truly are kick ass at what you do! We spent plenty of nights working on this book and I know I frustrated you to no end with my anti-outline writing style but don't give up on me, I'll get it together. LOL! Azarel, I will continue to thank you for taking a chance on me and believing in me until I take my last breath. I don't know if other publisher's take the time out to actually talk to their authors but I appreciate the fact that you do. Kelli, Necole, Cheryl, Winter, Tasha and the rest of the LCB family, thanks for the awesome book cover, editing, and constant love. Authors, Miss KP and C. Flores thanks for pushing my book…Kisses. I'm team LCB all day, every day.

There are a few people I've met in the literary world that I have to send a special shout out to. The women of OOSA Bookclub, Tanisha Webb, K'wan and Brenda Hampton. Whether you know it or not, the information that I've received from you all has really helped me. I thank you for welcoming me and continuing to drop those daily gems of what not to do and I will continue to follow them.

Lastly, I have to thank my readers. Nothing makes me smile brighter than a great review or a reader enthusiastically going off about a character that I wrote about. I know I am still new in the game but I promise if you stick with me, it will only get better.

Follow me on twitter, Facebook and Instagram: @iamchrisrenee @lcbooks. I love connecting with my readers.

Muah,
Chris Renee

Chapter 1

He threw me forcefully against the closet door. His fingers pried my jaw apart as he slid his tongue in and out of my mouth. For several minutes our tongues moved in sync while we drank each other's saliva, mad from thirst.

As I exhaled a deep moan, he inhaled it without a second thought. His chest swelled as the air forced his lungs to capacity. His right hand held my throat in a tight grip as his left hand moved up the side of my ample thighs and pushed my skirt around my waist.

Wearing panties was never my thing so he used that to his advantage. Eagerly, he pushed his thick fingers inside of me. "Ooh ahhooooooh," I murmured.

His eyes closed as a small smile of ecstasy washed past his lips. Those chocolate lips continued their assault upon my mouth, neck and all accessible skin. I ran my hands down his slim frame, searching to see what kind of package he was working with. I was excited to see that the night would completely be worth my time. It would take both of my hands to hold his most prized possession.

"Mmmm hmmm," he returned eagerly.

I glanced at the clock on the wall; it was already one o'clock in the morning. Even though I didn't have much time, I wasn't leaving until I completed what I'd come for. He had no idea what was in the making for him. My body was already tender to touch so I knew that it wouldn't be long before I received man's greatest gift to woman, a powerful orgasm. In my mind it was the only thing that most men were good for.

"Why don't you bend over and let me hit that ass from the back?" His baritone voice crooned while he continued to fondle me.

My heart raced, and with each palpitation, I sensed an intense burning. I wanted him inside of me. I had no further desire for his foreplay; there was no need to drag out the inevitable. I broke from our kiss and crawled onto the bed on all fours.

He nodded and smiled as he stroked the fabric, which held a firm imprint of his erection. He freed himself of his pants and shirt and then hopped behind me. He rushed to put his condom on with one hand as the other hand separated my ass cheeks. The first seconds of insertion swelled my insides. It only took a few strokes for our movements to become fluid. When I threw it back at him nastily, his knees buckled. His nails dug into my thighs causing me to slow my roll a little. I knew that would leave a mark on my peanut butter skin tone. I tried to shake his hands loose, but he still wouldn't let go.

"You like that?" he asked, as his pumps escalated into violent thrusts.

"I love it!" I replied.

"Awww, this shit is so good. I feel like I've died and gone to heaven. I'm about to bust," he whispered against my back.

"Not yet, luv. I'm gonna kill you softly tonight. No need to rush," I responded then slowed my grind.

I smiled with wicked intentions in my heart and allowed the euphoria to take control. He was messing up my moment with his eagerness. I liked to move at my own pace and so did my orgasm. In just a few seconds my mission would be complete. I wasn't leaving until he was drained of every last of inch of energy.

"Damn, girl, if this was the last snatch I ever got, it was damn sho worth it."

"Shut up and just keep going," I hissed at him.

My legs shook and the hair on the back of my neck stood at attention. It was time. I pushed him off me, flipped over and spread my toned legs high and wide as I placed my fingers on top of my throbbing clit. With my free hand, I motioned for him to come closer. I wanted him to watch the storm that he created. He needed to taste the nectar his sexual capabilities held.

"Open your mouth!" I ordered.

As he quickly obliged, the intense heat from his breath knocked down the levy that secured my orgasm. I grabbed his head and pushed him in closer. Loose tears poured from my eyes and spilled down my face. My spine throbbed but didn't deter me from my motive. I wrapped my golden brown thighs tighter around his neck in a death grip lock.

"W…Wait. Hold…up," he managed to say while trying to pry my thighs apart.

I knew he wanted me to stop. I also knew that the pressure was cutting off his circulation, but what he wanted didn't matter. My hips twisted violently as I drug his slender body back and forth like a rag doll. He was on the lighter side of the scale and I knew when I first met him that I pumped more iron in the gym than what he weighed soaking wet.

"Oh God, I'm coming! Shit!" I yelled between gasps of air.

While I was in a state of eternal bliss, my sex partner scratched both sides of my hips, desperately trying to free himself. I continued to hump his face intently and then cursed the inventors of sex as the orgasm ran its course. Nothing could stop me from relishing in the moment, not even the sudden sound of his neck snapping.

Mission accomplished, I thought to myself.

The cinnamon colored wig I was wearing slid off my head and hit the floor. I didn't even bother to adjust the hair net that secured my own long tresses from falling. I sat there for a few seconds, maybe longer, in order to gather my composure.

I stared into his bugged out eyes and smiled appreciatively for being broken off properly. Not only had that been one of the best sex sessions I ever had, but it was also the quickest. I pushed his now deceased corpse from between my thighs and hopped off the bed. It was already late so I only had a few minutes to clean up the mess and leave the scene without a trace.

I looked at his face again and shook my head in disappointment. He sure was one fine ass piece of man. With a thin mustache and a Caesar styled haircut, he reminded me of a darker version of the rapper, T.I. It was unfortunate that he was born to think with his dick and not his heart. Had he not been nothing more than a cheating bastard like most men were, he wouldn't have been in this situation. He thought he was clever, thinking his wife knew nothing about his secret apartment. He used this place to constantly break his wedding vows. His greed for lust had him blind, thinking that his wife was clueless. His bony ass even had the nerve to hit his wife from time to time when she drummed up the nerve to question him about his infidelity. If it was one thing in life that I despised the most, it was a man who used his wife as a punching bag.

I looked at him again in disgust. "Punk ass. You should've been a better man. Now, look at you." I desperately wanted to spit on his dead body, but couldn't leave any evidence behind, especially DNA.

Even though he was light as a feather when he was alive, his body had now turned to dead weight. I struggled to drag his heavy body across the floor and into the bathroom. I pushed him over into the tub and filled it with the bottles of bleach that I'd hidden earlier in the day when his wife gave me a copy of his key. I looked in the mirror to make sure I didn't have any noticeable marks on my neck. I didn't need the headache of having to explain a passion mark. I stared into my brown almond shaped eyes and was startled by the coldness that seemed to be behind them. I knew what the look was telling me, but I didn't want to deal with that shit at the moment, not when I still had work to do.

I pushed the image of my own face out of my head as I pulled a pair of surgical gloves out of my bag, and began to wipe the place clean. Anything I touched had to be wiped completely.

Minutes later, I cut the light off in the apartment and took out a black light to ensure that I removed all secretions. This was the part I hated the most. It took more time than the actual killing. One little mistake could wind up costing me my own life. It was a price that I no longer wanted to pay, but it paid the bills. Once I was sure the apartment was clean, I grabbed my cell phone and pressed the number two button on speed dial.

"It's done but I seriously don't know how much more of this I can take," I said wearily.

There was no response just a snort on the other end. I knew that snort all too well. It was filled with disappointment. I was expecting some kind of lecture about sticking the shit out but the call ended abruptly.

Tired and in need of a good night's sleep, I left the scene. As soon as I got home, I wasted no time hopping in the bed next to my husband, Jamison.

"How did it go tonight?" he asked me groggily.

"Umm…it was cool." I was quickly thrown off by his question since I thought he was asleep. "I took a lot of pictures that I know the magazine will like."

Turning over, he stared at me long and deep, which immediately made me uncomfortable. I nervously placed a kiss on his cheek to break the tension.

"Really? That's funny because you left your camera here," he replied.

I stared at him trying to think of an excuse, but couldn't convince my mouth to speak any of the lies that ran through my mind.

"By the way, I saw your dad today. He asked about you. You should go and see him, he's not looking too good," Jamison informed.

"Michael is dead," I mumbled angrily then turned over and buried my head under the comforter. I refused to call him my father since he didn't fill that role.

"He's not dead, Mykah. You can't run away from this problem for the rest of your life."

"Just drop that shit, Jamison!" I yelled firmly from under the covers.

Talking about the man who ruined my entire life was something that I didn't want to do. He was just as dead to me as the man whose life I'd just taken.

Chapter 2

"Good morning," Jamison greeted me from the kitchen table.

I could still feel the remnants of the previous night's mission between my thighs as I walked into the kitchen to prepare breakfast. I wanted nothing more than to stay curled under my covers all day and rest, but I tried to cook for my family whenever possible since I worked so much and was rarely around.

"Good morning," I said, leaning over to give him a sloppy kiss on his lips.

I hoped my kiss was a good way to apologize for my tardiness last night. Although he never came out and confronted me, I knew Jamison had a lot of questions about why I was always out late and away from home so much. Working the nightlife scene, shooting pictures for *Totally Chic* magazine was a great reason for me to be in the clubs, but sometimes I stayed out longer than the clubs were open. Even though he knew this, he was too proud to come off as insecure.

"Stop faking like you know your way around the kitchen, Mykah. I was just about to make breakfast but I got caught up on something. Just give me a second," Jamison said while stacking a bunch of papers.

"Look, I might not cook much anymore, but I still know how to crack a damn egg and make a good cheese omelet."

"Umm, I hate to kill your joy, but your omelets were never that great."

I stared at Jamison as he displayed a huge grin, showing off his full lips. Jamison was a manly man in every sense of the word. His solid 5'9 bronze frame was thick but firm thanks to good genes and former glory days on the football field in high school. Averaging over twenty-five hundred yards a season, he was St. Louis' top running back and a certified local celebrity during that time. As the *St. Louis American* often said, he was 'destined for stardom' after word got around that he'd been offered full scholarships to four different universities. However, Jamison surprisingly turned down his opportunity to go to college and the possibility to play in the NFL when he found out I was pregnant with twins. The entire city seemed to be disappointed about his decision. But no one was more pissed than his mother, Lucille. That woman hated the ground I walked on, and constantly blamed me for ruining her son's future.

She was so damn bitter that Jamison chose me over potential fame that she started drinking heavily to ease the pain of her son not becoming a Heisman Trophy winner and eventually the recipient of a multi-million dollar contract. In my opinion, the drinking habit was already there. She only used Jamison as an excuse to turn it up a notch. I would never forget the many times she showed up to his games drunk, yelling profanities at the referees the entire time.

The crazy part about it is that she used to love me when I was a kid. She was a good friend of my mother's. She was right there helping me become a young lady. It was all good until she noticed that Jamison and I had stopped looking at each other as brother and sister and more like lovers. Once her drinking problem increased, her hatred for me solidified. Whenever we were around each other she would address me as a whore, a huzzy or my all time favorite, a slutty cunt bitch. All of this normally happened right before she passed out in a drunken stupor. Nowadays Lucille was the certified neighborhood drunk; drinking anything she could get her hands on…daily.

"What…no smart response?" Jamison asked as I opened the refrigerator.

nice things. They're at an age where everything they want is expensive, and you know I want to give you things like that too so you won't have to keep wearing Tayla's hand-me-downs."

Tayla was my best friend. I often bought expensive things and lied to Jamison, telling him that they belonged to her.

"Look, I don't want to hurt your feelings but you would have to sell a shit load of books to be able to give us expensive things especially like the ones that Tayla's men give her."

"Damn, what crawled up your ass that quick? Why so negative?" Jamison asked angrily.

"Because I'm so fucking sick of you and these pipe dreams. Why don't you just get a real job like most men?"

I thought I said the last part in my mind, but somehow my voice had formed the words and said it out loud.

"Wow, so I don't make enough money for you now, Mykah? Never mind the fact that I gave up my dreams so that you wouldn't be pregnant and all alone, or shall I mention that if it wasn't for me you wouldn't have that lil' bullshit ass photography business of yours. I paid for that shit," he spat back at me.

"I'm sorry Jamison. I didn't mean it like that, but I'm just thinking realistically. What are the chances of you figuring out a case that the police can't even solve? That's all I'm saying."

"I hear what you saying. I just can't believe it, Mykah. You're talking real reckless to me like I don't handle my business around here. Hell, I even do your job as a mother since you're always too busy for the girls. You of all people should know how it feels to grow up without a mother. Why would you make our girls go through that? Thank God I'm not some sorry fuck up like your dad because then my girls would probably wind up like you."

I was furious. "You sorry piece of shit! How dare you mention my mother to try and hurt me? You know how I feel about that and for you to use that shit against me and imply that I'm not a good mother to them, that's low as hell."

My feelings were hurt that he would stoop so low. I felt bad enough for the missed time away from our daughters. I prayed they understood my reasoning for working so hard.

"Look, that was foul and I'm sorry. I'm just trying to fulfill my goals like you did when you started taking pictures. I need the support of my fucking wife if I'm going to ever live out my own dreams."

I knew it was wrong, far-fetched and petty of me to attack him for no reason. This argument made no sense whatsoever, but I couldn't back out of it. Distracting Jamison from this story was imperative.

"Look, just get a title that says, 'I'm thirty-three years old with a career,' not some little dream."

Jamison threw his hands up in frustration and looked at me as if I was the most ridiculous human he'd ever laid eyes on. Suddenly, a vein popped out the side of his neck. I watched the blood pump through it viciously. He was beyond mad.

"What's wrong with you, Mykah? Do you even hear yourself right now? Since you wanna bring up my age and what I'm not doing, you sound like some stupid ass little girl instead of a thirty-three year old woman yourself. So what? You're a damn local photographer." He clapped his hands loudly. "That's one hell of an accomplishment. I'm sure Donald Trump would be proud."

"Just leave me the hell alone, Jamison. This conversation is going further than it needs to."

I turned my attention back to the pancake batter that was all over the floor. I was so busy arguing with him I'd forgotten that I was supposed to be cooking. Jamison had pissed me off so bad that I wanted to pick up a frying pan and smash his head with it.

"You won't be here long enough for me to bother. You be in and out of this house like you a damn visitor."

"Listen, I said I'm done with this conversation before I really say some shit to hurt your feelings," I told him sternly.

"Yeah, you get real uncomfortable when the truth is in your face. You must think I'm some kind of fool. You bring your ass in the house late at night and try and sneak in the bed. Funny how you're at work all day, but you always smell like fresh soap when you creep in the house."

"And what the hell does that mean? Most men would actually like the fact that their wife smells good and furthermore what does that have to do with what we are talking about?" I asked.

"This has everything to do with the bad mood you've been in lately. I guess you really believe that I'm a fool. At least play the game with common sense."

"I don't know what you're talking about."

"You think I don't know what's going on but I know you're fucking around."

I was just about to respond to him when our seventeen-year-old twins unexcitedly came down the steps. Their long faces let me know they'd heard the entire argument. Sensing the tension in the air, they quickly grabbed their book bags and headed towards the back door.

"Hey, I was just about to make you girls something to eat," I said to them while plastering a fake Kool-Aid smile on my face. "Let me make y'all a quick bacon and egg sandwich."

"Nawl, we cool. I'm sure this little scene here is entertaining, but we're about to roll," Malia, the older of the two by sixty seconds responded snidely.

"Your dad is busy right now so I guess I'll be taking you guys to school," I told her.

I knew that Jasmine would more than likely not care one way or the other, but the decision would fall on Malia. Malia always played protector of Jasmine. Jasmine never made a move unless Malia approved it. The only free thought she had was in the way she dressed. Malia was a pink and lace type of girl while Jasmine preferred black and leather. Today was no different. Malia had on an all pink Victoria Secret sweat suit and Jasmine had on black leggings, a black studded shirt and a pair of Tory Burch ballerina flats I bought her for Christmas.

"Take us to school? We'll pass. We actually like driving to school ourselves," Malia said with an attitude.

"Drive? Don't be silly. You don't even have your license."

"Actually, Ma, we got our license last month. Daddy took us," Jasmine added quietly.

If it wasn't awkward enough in the kitchen, it had definitely turned that way with her revelation. I didn't even know they could drive let alone have their license already.

"Oh, I didn't know. No one tells me anything anymore," I said trying to save face.

"That's because you're barely here," Malia mumbled. *Out being a whore,* I thought I heard her say.

I chose to ignore her to keep the peace, but would surely check her ass later on when we were alone. That would have to be after I checked Jamison for not telling me about such a big milestone in their lives.

"Okay, well how about we hit the mall after school? The new Jordans came out today and I know y'all want them."

"That's okay, Daddy already got us the hook up with his connect. He got us a pair last week," Jasmine responded.

I was shocked that Jamison had that kind of pull from a connect that I knew nothing about. I glared at him before turning my attention back to the twins. They'd really grown into beautiful young women that would definitely give any man a run for his money later in life. They were identical with cocoa smooth skin, high cheek bones, long natural chin length hair that was normally parted down the middle; and thick, voluptuous bodies that developed way too soon. They looked so much like me that it was somewhat scary, even down to the mole that sat under all three of our left eyes. People often said that the three of us looked like triplets, except I'd recently cut bangs into my shoulder length hair. I guess one could call it good genes since I looked so young myself. We were only sixteen years apart and I felt more like their sister than their mother at times.

"Okay, well how about a pamper day then? Get your hair and nails done and I know a place that gives the best massages. I just need a little time, that's all," I begged slightly.

"That sounds fun. I'm game," Jasmine said in surprise.

I looked at Malia for a response, but she just rolled her light brown eyes at me and took a bite from the banana in her hand.

Malia seemed to be smelling herself lately but Jasmine was still in my corner. I would never say it out loud but she was my favorite of the two. Malia cleared her throat and gave Jasmine a stern look. The silent twin code they had always drove me nuts. I wondered what the two of them were up to.

"We can't do that. Time is priceless…reserved for the worthy," Malia said as they both strutted to the door.

She stopped in her tracks and turned towards Jamison. She hugged him tightly and encouraged Jasmine as well. I opened my arms expecting the same thing, but I was shit out of luck. They ran out of the door without giving me a second thought. I stood there with my mouth open as I tried to put together what happened.

Did they just blatantly ignore me? I thought to myself.

Jamison snickered as he looked at the shock I wore firmly upon my face. My heart was broken and I was certain he told the twins something bad about me to make them mad at me.

"So you have to bribe your girls into liking you more?"

"I don't have to tell them shit. They can see you for what you really are. Hell, we all can see it. Maybe you forgot or maybe you just don't give a damn anymore but you missed another one of their recitals last night."

"Shit," I quickly said to myself.

It had totally slipped my mind. No wonder they were so pissed at me. I promised not to miss one like I'd done with the previous ones. I instantly felt like shit. Maybe I was a bad mother.

"Yeah, that's right, you were mysteriously unavailable. But I can guess where you were based on those bruises you rocking up and down your thighs."

I looked down at my legs and couldn't believe what I saw. I silently cursed again at myself for not covering my tracks in a more thorough manner. I hadn't noticed I was bruised when I used the bathroom earlier. Not only were there bruises, those I could easily explain as bumping into something, but there were scratch marks on them as well. I glanced at Jamison and struggled to get out a suitable excuse but nothing came to mind.

"Jamison, it's not what you think, I swear."

"I'm over this shit, Mykah, and I can promise you that if I walk out that door, I'm taking my girls with me. I did everything that I was supposed to as a husband and you continue to make a fool out of me. It's funny that you can't even see that you're just like your fucking father," he said before turning around and storming out of the kitchen.

I started to follow him and continue our argument when my phone vibrated alerting me of a new text message. I opened it up and saw a picture of me walking in the parking lot last night. I completely freaked out when I saw the next picture that included me and the man that I killed. I looked frantically at the phone for the number of the sender, but it was all zeros.

I looked over my shoulder to make sure Jamison wasn't in the room before quickly deleting the evidence. I had to find out who was following me before my husband found out what I was into or even worse…the police.

Chapter 3

I didn't trust her from the moment she sashayed her little pint-sized, toned ass in my office. As soon as my door opened and the bell chimed, I could tell that I didn't like her nor would I ever get to like her. Call it a woman's intuition. As cliché as that sounds, that feeling is right most of the time. A strange sensation in my stomach flip-flopped easily rivaling Gabby Douglas in a tumbling match.

I was still unnerved by the argument with Jamison. Something in him was different and I couldn't figure out what. The fact that my girls were possibly looking at me like I looked at Michael when I was their age, crushed me even further. And the mysterious text messages did nothing to help this fucked up day I was having. I couldn't figure out who would've sent that to me when I was so careful in making sure I covered my tracks. Something was definitely off in my universe and the scales were about to tip closer to disaster with whoever Ms. Thang was.

"Are you Mykah, the girl that I'm looking for?" she asked me in a high nasally tone.

"The woman that you're looking for," I corrected her.

She laughed and my nerves flopped once again. There was something sinister about her laughter. My guess was if the devil had decided to walk the earth, he used her chocolate frame to do his bidding. Even though she was breathtakingly beautiful, I could still see the evil behind her cold gray eyes. Very odd to see those eyes on a black woman, they were contacts, I concluded. Whatever they were, they spooked the hell out of me, but somehow had the capability to hypnotize me at the same time.

"Is this how you treat all your potential clients?" she asked.

"It all depends on the client. What can I do for you? Are you interested in a wedding package?"

She looked up at the huge photo of a bride that hung on the wall behind my desk. In spite of my mind screaming, *get her the hell out of here*, I figured I would entertain her because I could smell her money a mile away. And believe me, she reeked of old wealth. There was a big difference between old wealth and new showboat, temporary money that athletes and singers lucked into. They would waste their money on all useless things just to say, look at me now, but would be flat broke in a couple of years. The fact that it happened more often than not blew my mind.

Don't get me wrong though, she was draped in designer clothes from head to toe, but you wouldn't know the labels unless it was your own everyday gear, or your obsession to obtain it. I sat somewhere in between the middle of those categories, shopping for my designer clothes at discount stores like Nordstrom Rack or Last Call by Neiman Marcus, but that was only to live a modest middle class life like Jamison wanted because I really had more than enough money to floss on a daily.

"I'm already married," she said disgustedly, and then flashed what appeared to be at least a four carat princess cut ring.

Her pointy nose turned at the corners as she moved closer to me and frowned at the décor in the office. She even had the nerve to remove a container of Lysol wipes from her obnoxiously expensive black Python Celine bag, and proceeded to wipe the invisible dirt from my leather chair before she sat down across from me.

I snorted my nose and held my tongue from calling her a bitch as I knew she deserved. After all, it seemed to me that she was trying to piss in front of me to mark her territory. We had a momentary stare down before she cleared her throat and spoke in a soft but forceful tone.

"I want you to kill my husband," she said bluntly.

"I'm sorry?"

I was totally taken aback by her boldness. Okay, so I was paid to kill men for a living, but how about a little small talk before we jump straight onto the path of hell together. I always made it a rule to know what level of evil I dealt with beforehand.

That was the first rule that Lady taught me when she decided to initiate me into the game she used to play. I turned to her when the bill collectors would not stop calling our house a year after Jamison stopped working. With our house in foreclosure, I had no other choice but to agree to her terms of a loan. She gave me fifty thousand dollars and sent me to a slew of strenuous self-defense classes including Tae Kwon Do. I had the best black belt instructor in St. Louis teaching me all the moves you see on T.V. which didn't take long for me to master. I assumed that was the hard part, but the mental aspects of learning what Lady knew almost broke me down. She taught me to trust no one, especially not men, not even Jamison. I had to shut my heart off completely, but Jamison was always able to crack through it every now and then.

"Ugh, hello? I asked if you were the woman who could kill my husband?" the woman said loudly, pulling me from my drifting thoughts.

"Umm sorry. I don't know what you're talking about," I said, typing a few things into my computer.

"Look, I don't have time to play games. I heard you were the woman for the job. I need my husband dead. So, will you kill him or not?"

I looked around nervously. I thought maybe the Feds were on to me and this was a set up. I never conducted business of this nature at the office, but this perfectly beautiful woman sat before me. I couldn't help but have a tiny ounce of jealousy because the bitch looked more like a beauty queen instead of some whack job who was dressed to the nines and wandered into my office uninvited. I was just online eyeing the spring 2014 Prada heels that she wore. Her clothes were crisp and heavily starched. I wanted to find something on her that was in some form of disarray but I couldn't find anything.

"I'm not sure where you have gathered your information from Mrs…" I paused and waited for her to give me her name.

"Mrs. Chauntelle LaRue, but not for long if I can help it," she added quickly.

I lifted my eyebrow at the last name of LaRue. They were a notorious family whose dirty money was cleaned up in politics and payoffs. They ran St. Louis behind the scenes and ruled the city like an army. Some were clean law abiding citizens, but you never knew which you were dealing with until it was too late. I had to be really careful with how I handled this.

"Who told you I was the woman you were looking for?"

"Look, word gets around. I'm friends with the wife of the late, Thomas Early. She told me you knocked her husband off for a couple hundred thousand. I have more to offer than that. I'll give you one million dollars plus a fifty thousand dollar agreement bonus."

Hearing the amount she was offering caused me to sit up straighter in the chair. *She must really be desperate,* I thought.

Thomas was the guy I'd gotten rid of the night before. Even though his wife had wired the remaining fifty thousand dollar fee into my secret personal account this morning, she had no right to tell this woman what I did for her. That shit was part of the deal.

My account was another secret I kept from Jamison. I would put what I considered the standard pay for a photographer in our joint account whenever I had an assignment and he remained oblivious to how much money I really had. The thought of getting one million dollars really intrigued me. This was a once in a lifetime opportunity. I could flip a million dollars a million different ways and be set for life.

"Have you talked to Lady?" I asked her.

"Who?" she replied with an attitude.

Lady was always the middleman in all of my transactions. I didn't know the women who were sent to me. The common denominator was always the fact that we knew Lady. The women were all sworn to secrecy so I was a bit ticked off that one of them sent this woman my way. I would have to speak to Lady because there was something about this situation that I just did not trust.

"Are you the police?" I questioned her.

"Chile please. Hell no, I'm not the police. Do you know who I'm married to?"

"You don't look like the type of woman who would get involved in something like this."

"And you don't look like the type of woman who could lure rich and powerful men towards you and then kill them."

I took the dig that she threw at me with a slight smile. I was used to model thin, pretty girls like her. She thought she was better than me. She assumed her enhanced looks were superior to my natural features. Little Miss Perfect who could pull any man she wanted, didn't think that I could compete with the likes of her.

"I'm going to need you to strip down. Shake your hair out, and empty that nice hand bag of yours on my desk," I said calmly.

"What the hell? You can't possibly expect for me to get naked in this office?"

She waved her frail manicured hand around in the air. I stifled a laugh at her horror. I knew the request was over the top, but I wanted to bring her down a few pegs. Women like her deserved it.

"My services, my rules. You can either take them or walk your little prissy ass out the same way you came in," I said nonchalantly as I began to type on my computer again.

She sighed before quickly discarding her clothes. She shook the loose curls from her long, ombre colored hair. It was done so nicely that I couldn't tell if it was weave or her real hair. Once she turned the bag over and dumped it, I smiled at the amount of money held together nicely by rubber bands. The obnoxiously catchy rap song, *Bands A Make Her Dance*, jingled in my ears.

"Happy now?" she asked with an attitude.

Hell no, I wasn't happy at all! Seeing her flat abs and frail body without a single inch of fat only made me wish I'd skipped lunch earlier and all the days before. Even though I hit the gym every other day, my shit wasn't stacked up like hers. However, the ridiculousness of the situation did tickle my happy bone a smidget. Had she not been so rude she wouldn't be standing there looking like a damn fool. I fixed the smirk on my face and tried to remain professional.

"Yes, I am. Now, what were you saying?"

She shot me a mean look as she slipped back into her clothes, but her attitude seemed to have readjusted a tiny bit. Humiliation was a well-put-together woman's worst nightmare.

"I need my husband dead. I thought about leaving him, but I know I wouldn't get a dime of his money. After the pain and suffering I've gone through, I need compensation, major compensation."

"Listen, I wouldn't just kill a man because his wife is not getting her way. You're gonna have to dig deeper than that."

"He's a cheater, liar, manipulator, and I can go on all day about what makes him an asshole."

"What's your husband's name?"

She paused and looked to be considering trusting me. Her suspicions were all over her face. Little did she know, the feeling was very mutual.

"My husband is Dyson LaRue."

Dyson fell in that pot of downright crooked LaRues. He was a hothead rich kid who had everything without working hard for it, but always had to prove his manhood unnecessarily. A few years back he was on trial for executing four men in a boardroom meeting. He was miraculously acquitted on all charges when each witness disappeared. Word had it that his family paid off the judges, the witnesses, and the jury.

"Mrs. LaRue, you do realize what you're asking me is considered a capital offense, right? Not only that, your husband is a part of a legendary brutal family."

I needed to make sure she knew if we ever got caught, the state of Missouri wouldn't feel guilty offering us the death penalty, which would be the lesser of two evils, considering that if the LaRue family ever found out, we both would be tortured and killed in a horrible manner.

"I'm not here for a damn lecture. Now if you're already thinking about getting caught, maybe you aren't the woman for the job," she replied with her snooty ass voice. "And call me, Chauntelle. That Mrs. LaRue shit sounds too old."

"I can handle mine. I just want to make sure you're certain. Are you?"

I had to ask her again because I knew a scorned woman was a highly emotional person. I didn't want her to regret this later on and then confess to someone.

"Yes, I'm sure. Without having to go into too much of my business, I was young, broke and desperate when I met Dyson. I needed money so I married him. It was the worst mistake I could ever make. I married the devil and he said the only way out was death. I would prefer him to be dead and not me."

Chauntelle seemed to have relaxed for the first time since she walked through the door. She opened a pouch inside of her handbag and pulled out a cigarette and a lighter that was shaped like a tube of lipstick. She looked at me for approval until I nodded my head. The calmer her nerves were, the more information I would be able to gather.

I allowed her to have a few seconds of relief as she inhaled the smoke and smiled. Her eyes had softened and became more beautiful than my first glance at them. I saw the vulnerability behind them. And for the first time I felt sorry for her.

"I don't personally know your husband, only what I read in the papers or through rumors. Would you consider him a dangerous man?"

"Dangerous would be too nice of a word for the likes of him." Chauntelle blew tiny o's with her smoke.

"Has he ever hit you?" I asked her softly.

"Please, he's not the type of man to hit a woman. He's a total Mama's boy. Now his goons, bodyguards or whatever you want to call them, they will beat the hell out of me whenever he tells them too," she replied absently.

The pain she felt washed over her and I knew that I would have to help her out of the situation. No woman deserved to be beaten and forced to stay with a man because she fears he'll kill her if she leaves.

"How many of these people does he carry around with him?"

"I don't know, they're everywhere, watching and following people. They probably know I'm here now."

Upon hearing her statement, I looked out of the window at the parking lot. Nothing seemed unusual, but at the mention of his goons, she seemed to be spooked.

"You think someone actually followed you here?"

"Maybe we should just forget this. I'm sorry, I should have never come." She stood in a hurry and walked away to leave. I should've let her go on about her business, but my heart really felt for her, plus her damn money was still calling my name. I normally charged two hundred grand, so a million dollars was the biggest payoff I'd ever been offered. With that kind of money, Dyson would surely be my last assignment and then I could focus on my family. I would make up some excuse about inheriting a large sum of money and then we could live happily ever after. I now realized that Chauntelle was actually the answer to my prayers.

"Wait, I'll help you. I'll take the assignment," I called after her.

She stopped midway to the door and spun around towards me.

"Why are you so eager all of a sudden?" she asked suspiciously.

"You think, as a woman, that I would be able to go home and not worry that one day his 'goons' will kill you?

I'm not made like that. You got the wrong one. Now, do you want to get this bastard back and take all he has at the same time?" I asked her in the hardened tone I used whenever I was speaking with my kids. She seemed like a little girl to me. She was like a frail porcelain doll with perky breasts and wrinkle-free skin. I didn't get her age, but I knew that we weren't that far apart from each other.

"Now you're speaking my language, money. I know that fluently, and I'm very serious about it. Money is the one thing that I will not play about," she replied firmly.

Reaching in her purse, Chauntelle threw three huge stacks of bills on my desk, each with a $50,000 yellow band around it. Then she gave me a piece of paper that I assumed was her husband's personal information. Quickly skimming over the money, I was happy she'd given me something solid to start with.

"It's been nice meeting you, Mykah. Consider this a down payment, but remember what I said about people playing with my money." She paused, and slid her Tom Ford sunglasses onto her face.

"Likewise, Chauntelle, I will be contacting you soon. I don't normally conduct this kind of business here so feel free not to come back."

"That lil' fact will be noted. Here's one for you, I will walk through hell and fight the devil tooth and nail about my money. It's best you be mindful of what I said," she hissed my way.

Chauntelle turned sharply and walked out of my office before I could respond. I probably wouldn't have said anything anyway. There was something about her that made me feel as if she had already been to hell and back before. I could have sworn I saw smoke in her trail.

Chapter 4

The next few days were quite uneventful as I gathered as much information as possible on Dyson LaRue. I knew his family grew up in the projects downtown. Our families grew up in the same area so I knew it well.

I actually had the perfect person to speak to who would have all the information I needed on Dyson, but I knew that she would be pissed that she was cut out of the deal. Lady always received twenty percent commission, a referral fee, on all of my hits. I would have to bribe her with liquor in order to make her forget about that. It was true that Lady didn't play about her money. She once told me that she called the state on a woman who owed her money back in the day. She lied and said that the woman was not treating her kids right. The state eventually came and took the kids. I guess Lady didn't give a damn about tearing the family apart. Even knowing all that, I knew that the only thing that she loved just as much as her money was her liquor.

I grabbed a bottle of Courvoisier and started the short trip over to the senior citizen high-rise building. Lady always played bingo there. I knew that she would be there with her bingo stampers, her cup and her attitude. Lady didn't live there full time, but she had enough pull wherever there were beating hearts. She kept an apartment on the fourth floor just so some of her good for nothing grandkids would have a place to stay. As long as they kept quiet the director let Lady pay him a little extra not to tell that young people lived there.

Lady didn't get out much but when she did it was only to the bingo hall, the casino and occasionally she would be on the corner shooting craps with the local hoodlums. She used all three places to get her daily dose of gossip. Even though Lady had enough money to move somewhere down south and live a peaceful life, it was obvious that she could never leave the projects.

She walked those streets in the name of civil rights, raised her kids there, and made it through the devastation of unsafe times in the projects. Anyone who was born before or after her, whose feet hit those same streets, knew to treat her with the highest form of respect. She was quick to go upside anybody's head and if that wasn't enough, she had a slew of knucklehead grandkids, boys and girls, who wouldn't hesitate to turn up in a heartbeat.

Back in her day, Lady was one of the coldest boosters St. Louis had ever seen. Her clientele included the pimps, hustlers, whores, movers and shakers. Nothing went down underground without Lady knowing firsthand.

As soon as I walked into the building, I resisted my urge to gag from the smell of old people and mothballs. I would've thought I was pregnant the way my stomach lurched back and forth, but I'd secretly gotten my tubes tied when I decided to work with Lady. Sleeping with other men was one thing, but to get pregnant by one would probably be unforgivable. Even though I required each of them to wear condoms, I still didn't want to take that chance. I tucked that into my file of secrets that Jamison would never know about. He'd been begging me for years to try for a son, but that was never going to happen. I was done with kids.

"B 51," the announcer called out.

"What was that?" A tiny white woman said in the front of the room. She had hearing aids in both of her ears.

"Damn it, Maybelene! Don't start this shit today! You fuckin' up my game," Lady's voice rang out. "B 51!"

I searched the room and found Lady and her slanted blonde wig sitting in the back by herself with her table covered with bingo cards. She moved fast, feeling across each card for the number that was called. Lady's eyesight was fucked up so she kept a pair of fake Chanel shades on her face to block anyone from looking into her eyes.

I sat next to her quietly and watched in amazement as she worked each card. I grabbed her cup and poured until it was full to the rim. She paused momentarily and inhaled deeply, allowing the smell of the liquor to serenade her nose. She shot back into action and impatiently waited on the next number to be called only for someone else to yell out 'Bingo!' She shook her head, grabbed the cup, and took a long deep gulp. She involuntarily shimmied to the side as the liquor heated her body.

"What you want, Mykah?" Lady asked as she regained her composure.

Her style was sharp as hell as she sat there in black skinny jeans and a see through black shirt with a wide zebra print collar. Her red studded bra may have been bedazzled by one of her grandkids because I seriously doubted if she'd bought it that way.

"What's up, Lady? How you been?" I asked, trying to make it seem like I didn't only come for information. I really did love her with all my heart.

"You may attract more bees with honey, but I'm a fly, Sugar. So give me the shit straight and funky, just how I like it. And hurry up cause we only have five minutes 'fore the next game starts," Lady replied as she continued to drink with one hand and swooped her blonde bangs from her forehead with the other. It was hilarious how her blonde wigs never fit her head.

Lady sucked on the gold tooth that she refused to get rid of. I chuckled slightly because she always came up with several classic one-liners. They made her the most quoted woman in the hood, but I knew them on more of a personal level. Lady and my mother grew up together and had been nothing but the best of friends until my mother died in a car accident. My mother was more than likely high off of antidepressants the night she left in search for my father at his mistress' house. I would never forget watching her speed off in her car that night. I was devastated when she passed away. Had it not been for Lady stepping up to the plate and literally becoming my second mother, I wouldn't have survived. I owed her my life for that.

Michael became so depressed after my mother died that he spent most of his time drunk. Ridden with guilt all he did was sulk. He was the reason that she died and I hated him for that. I prayed every night for years that the police would find him dead somewhere. Unfortunately, my prayers were never answered.

I heard through Lady a while back that he had some big ass epiphany and turned his rotten soul over to the Lord and became a pastor. That was the biggest joke I'd ever heard and one of the reasons why I didn't get the whole "church thing". How could someone so evil, who spent most of his time making his wife and child miserable, become a changed man? Should all of his sins be forgiven? Apparently God forgives, but I didn't have any plans of trying to. Each man that I killed had selfish, manipulative qualities just as Michael had, which is why they were easily disposable.

"Well, spit it out. Already told you I ain't got all day," Lady said.

"I got a new client and he's a little slippery. I need to really be on point with this one. No room for errors at all."

She paused and seemed to be processing my words. I knew she was wondering how someone got to me without going through her. Lady was always suspicious of everything and everyone.

"What you mean, you got a new client? How the hell did that happen?"

"She just showed up at the office. She said Mrs. Early put her onto me. I thought you said none of the women we dealt with would talk."

"How the hell you just let some unknown woman pop up and you discuss business wit' her? She probably the damn police. I oughta put yo' dumb ass out of here for bringin' the heat my way," Lady replied angrily.

"Look, the woman showing up is your fault."

"My fault?"

"Yeah, your fault, Lady. Your referral ran her damn mouth and now I have to help this woman so she won't go babbling what she knows to the police."

I hadn't even thought of that before coming to see Lady, but it was a great way to divert her attention away from the fact that I was going to freelance the assignment.

"Ain't shit my fault lil' girl. And don't you worry 'bout no loose mouths. I got some gorilla glue that will keep shit shut. Trust me; I'll have a stern talk with Mrs. Early. By the way, how did that go?"

I looked around to make sure no one was in our conversation. "It went well. Just like all the rest."

Lady took the last sip of cognac. "Good. Now, who could possibly be unlucky enough to have yo' unwanted attention?"

Lady waved the now empty cup in my direction and I hurriedly poured the remainder of the contents into it. I hadn't gotten any useful information yet and she was almost done with her poison of choice. I cursed myself inwardly for not getting a bigger bottle.

I leaned closer to Lady so I could whisper in her ear. The LaRues did a lot for the community and I didn't want any of their supporters to overhear me talking bad about him.

"It's Dyson LaRue. I got a little bit of information about him, but now I need the underground info. He moves slick as hair grease so I know gathering anymore info is gonna be harder than I think."

She stopped moving and didn't even take a drink from her cup. I thought she might have passed out behind those dark shades when she suddenly responded in an empty voice.

"Now you about to step into a pretty deep sinkhole full of shit messin' 'round wit' them LaRues, lil' girl. They don't play fair at all and they for damn sure don't keep enemies alive to talk about it. That rotten Preston LaRue, the head of the family, runs his ship pretty damn tight. He'd kill and eat one of his own kin if his fat ass was hungry," she warned me.

"I really need this money. She's offering a half of a million dollars and it's probably the only chance I will get to shake out of this business. Jamison been acting kind of strange lately and the girls are getting tired of me not being around, especially Malia. Her attitude towards me seems to get worse by the day. I need to chill and get my family right. The money I've saved is more than enough to get me out of the game. I'm just sick of this shit, anyway, Lady. I keep telling you that and it's like you don't hear me. The smell of death is embedded in my damn nose. I need this money so I can be done. You know how it is."

"I may know how it is but yo' lil' nappy head ass always been hardheaded, just like yo' damn daddy. Since I know you already done made yo' mind up, I'm gone help you, but when them still waters get real deep, don't come round here lookin' for me to throw out no life jacket. And I betta get my regular twenty percent, plus ten more because you on some snake shit."

My eyes widened. "Thirty percent…for what? Damn, I didn't expect you to try and beat me over my head."

I was a little irked by her greediness. I'd always given her money without question and treated her like a true mother, but this time she wasn't doing anything to warrant a percentage.

"How you gone come up in here, fuckin' up my groove, askin' for my resources but don't wanna give me a cut? On top of all that, this shit could really bring some heat down on us. You got some nerve, lil' girl."

"I'm just saying, this ain't personal, just business. You weren't the connect on this. You told me to always put business before personal," I said to her.

"Oh okay, I see. You tryin' to use my own shit on me, huh? You tryin' to play big girl chess now, Mykah? You better damn well know, what goes over the camel's back got to go up under his stomach."

Lady's words were sharp and intended to cut through my bones. I didn't know what the hell she was talking about and I would never admit it to her, but she scared me.

"What camel? I don't know what you talking about," I replied in confusion.

I thought maybe the alcohol had already kicked in, but I also knew that Lady was a damn good drinker. It would take more than some tiny bottle to get her drunk.

"What goes the fuck around comes back the fuck around, that's what I'm sayin'," she said through clenched teeth. "I put you into this game, and I can take you out of it, too. You better play right."

I stared at her gold tooth that she shined so good that I could see my reflection in it.

"Alright, Lady, is five percent cool? Besides, I can't do it without your help anyway," I reassured her then kissed her cheek. "I love you, Lady."

She didn't respond, instead she said, "I'm glad you came around to yo' senses. Look, I'm gonna help you get to Dyson, Mykah but you better not ever mention my name to those LaRues."

"Now why would I do something like that? Trust me, no one will know a thing as always."

"They better damn well not. I love you, but if it comes down between the two of us, I will be cryin' and mournin' at yo' funeral. And I hope you know I'm gone show my natural black ass and fall all over the casket actin' a fool."

"I understand, so lay it on me," I said while laughing.

"You sure? Because I don't want no shit," Lady stated again.

"Please, Lady, just tell me what you know so I can get outta here."

"Now a couple weeks ago, maybe on a Sunday, I'm sure it probably was Sunday cause I made them pinto beans and ham hocks for dinner and they tore my stomach up somethin' terrible. Anyway, I asked that no good grandson of mine to go get me some Bismo to settle it some, but he done disappeared, and more than likely was up in that damn crack house gettin' high or maybe over his no good baby momma house. He never gave me a straight answer on where he was that night," she rambled on and on.

I tapped my nails impatiently on the table and tried to draw her back to the moral of the story but she was already in her own world, taking her time.

"So, like I was sayin', I heads out on my own to get some Bismo from the corner store and on my way back I sees this slick silver car parked on the side of the high rises. It was one of those Mercedes Benz's. Now, it ain't often those kinds of cars just happen to be in the hood without some fanfare from the local hoodrats, so I found it mighty suspicious. I laid low in the cut and watched as Suzette's daughter, you know that real loose and stank one, Asia, walks past the car. The door opens and out comes the youngest one, Dyson. I couldn't hear real good what they were sayin', somethin' 'bout missing money from his club. They was damn sure arguin' and then he whistles and his big black friend gets out the front of the car and gives her one hard punch to the face, knocking her out cold. They toss her in the trunk and sped off. Ain't nobody seen that chile since. Her Mama over there baldhead worryin' herself about it."

I already knew Dyson was dangerous but hearing stories about things he did sent a chill through me. *Would killing him really be worth risking my life?* The thought passed through my mind, but was quickly washed away by the faces of my girls in the kitchen the other day. I had to pursue this option.

"What you think they did with her?" I asked.

"Well, word is that LaRue is runnin' a side hustle of turnin' women into sex slaves for his lil' politician friends and who knows who else. He just auctions them up like they cattle or somethin'. That's one evil man. He ain't wrapped too tight if you ask me and I thank God he wasn't round when I was out there," she replied to me in a slurred tone.

Sex slaves? I questioned inside my head. This was a whole new territory for me, but it also presented itself as being my way to get closer to him. I knew sex if I didn't know anything else.

"You know where the auctions take place? How I can get in good with him?"

Lady pushed her sunglasses down on her nose and it surprised me because out of all the years I'd known her, I'd never seen her eyes before. They were a hazel brown and absolutely beautiful. She looked at me sternly and then slipped the glasses back up.

"I don't know shit. Now gone and get yo' lil' unlucky ass out of here. I was on my way to winnin' fore you come in here jinxin' me," Lady said as she put her focus back on the new cards.

"G-11," the announcer called out.

I smiled, realizing she knew how but didn't want me involved with Dyson. However, desperate times caused for desperate measures. I had to make her believe that I wasn't afraid. The more I convinced her, the more I would convince myself.

"Alright, Lady, I'm out of here. You only kicking me out because I'm out of liquor but I still love you though," I said, gathering my things. I stood up to leave.

"Next time you come around here tryin' to get my damn panties wet, you gone have to bring a bigger bottle. I ain't no cheap hoe."

Just when I was about to leave, she grabbed my arm and dug her dingy nails into my skin. She pulled me so close I could've drank the cognac from her tongue.

"Whatever, but you be careful with this one. I know Chauntelle is the one who want him gone and she just as evil as he is. Her crazy ass sliced her brother up when she was a youngin, lied and said he'd been touchin' on her. She was just jealous, thought her parents gave him too much attention. That bitch a cold piece of work," Lady ended, warning me a final time with a final shoo of her hand.

I knew my instincts were right about something being off about Chauntelle. If she could do something like that to her own flesh and blood, she wouldn't hesitate to get rid of someone not related. I tried to wash away my fear with a laugh as if Lady told me a joke.

"I got this, Lady. I've been doing this a while now and I'm very thorough with mine. I've faced men ten times worse than Dyson and his wife. However, I appreciate the love your mean self shows me. It means a lot to me but I have to go."

"Don't forget about that business you have to handle tonight," she said.

I'd forgotten all about it because I was so caught up in the hype of this new case. Plus, the new target was so damn boring that I dreaded having to spend any time with him.

"Now you know I never forget anything. I'll call you when I'm done," I replied.

"And call yo' damn daddy. He wants to see you. I think you will regret not talkin' to him!" she yelled at me.

I stopped moving and stared at her. She knew better than anyone that I didn't want to hear shit about that man. It was because of him that my mother and her best friend were dead. I had no conversation for that man no matter what he wanted.

"I don't have shit to say to him, Lady. You know that."

I pushed my hair out of my face and rolled my eyes at her. She had managed to irk me by bringing this dude up.

"You better get that damn tiger out yo' throat and relax them eyes lil' girl. You gettin' beside yourself. How long you gonna hold on to some shit that happened years ago? That hatred is gonna eat yo' ass alive. Yo' father is sick so that should make some type of damn difference. Now, get yo' ass outta here."

I looked at Lady in disbelief and was about to walk away, but I needed to ask her one more question, and I hoped she wouldn't become offended by it.

"Lady, how do you see everything that happens and you're blind?"

She chuckled and looked at me, but it felt like she was looking through me.

"I mind my business and you mind yours, lil' girl," she replied and then gave her full attention back to her bingo cards.

Moments later, I walked out of the door and looked around. For some strange reason, it felt like I was being watched. But I brushed it off as being paranoid from Lady warning me and kept it moving. After walking to my truck, I opened the door. As soon as I got in, a silver Mercedes CLS with tinted windows flew past, so close, it almost tore my door off in the process.

"Shit!" I yelled out as the car speed away.

I sat there for a few seconds trying to calm my nerves before quickly starting my car. The kids in this area were always speeding, so all I could do was thank my lucky stars I didn't get hit, or God forbid, they hit my new truck. It took a great deal of convincing Jamison that we could keep up the payments on our Porsche Cayenne, so I didn't want a single scratch on it. I was just about to put the truck in drive when my phone chimed back to back, notifying me of two new text messages.

Washington Avenue: where home life and nightlife meets, no sign or nothing.

I smiled at Lady's message. I knew she would come through for me with Dyson's whereabouts, but my feeling of cloud nine was short lived. As soon as I went to the next message, my heart was surrounded with fear.

You may wanna be careful getting in your car. Wouldn't want you dying before you see what kind of hell you're about to go through.

I dropped the phone and went for the small .25 caliber I kept under the seat. I looked around before quickly speeding off. Whoever was harassing me was getting out of control. I had no clue on who it could be and that was to their advantage, but I had a pacemaker made of steel for their ass.

Chapter 5

I looked around at the dingy motel room. I even tried to think of one thing nice to say about the room but the only thing I could come up with was the walls and the bed sheets matched in pee stain yellow. The television was missing from the stand and I saw the faint outlining of a left over body chalk on the floor. This was an all time low for me. Most of my targets liked the finer things in life, but this cheap bastard was not the norm.

"You feel so soft," he moaned in my ear.

I held him in a firm hug and rolled my eyes behind his back. He felt like shit to me, nothing more than just another paycheck. I tried to take his jacket off, but he stopped my hands from moving. I'd never been in a situation where the man refused to take all of his clothes off. Ass naked with a jacket on made me wonder what he was hiding. I had to force myself to pretend that he was my celebrity crush, Idris Elba.

"You feel good, too, Daddy. Give it to me just like that," I moaned in return.

He placed kisses up and down my neck as he continued to take his time inside of me. He was the type of man who liked to drink and make love to everyone but his wife. Everything about him reminded me of the coward of a man that made me. His wife was just as frantic as my mother used to be, but she was snobby and shrewd. She knew her husband had been cheating for years, but due to his heavy drinking he'd become verbally abusive to her and her son. She couldn't take it anymore and hired me to take her out of her misery.

"Got damn, baby. I need to buy you something after this. Shit, as good as this pussy feels you can have all my damn money."

I rolled my eyes again because I highly doubted that his cheap ass would be giving me anything. According to his wife they were living the high life, but yet we were rolling around in someone else's STD stained sheets.

"I'll hold you to that," I said.

"Say, Daddy, why don't you lay back on the bed and let me ride you to sleep?"

He was out of breath and looked like he was near the brink of death without my assistance. Slobber dribbled down the side of his cheek, mixing in with his salt and pepper beard. Sweat poured from his balding head, causing his bad black dye job to run on the sides of his face and forehead. It made him look demented.

"Good idea. If you want some change for your pocket book, you gone have to work for it."

I laughed because he had no idea how true his words were. I was working hard for it, but it for damn sure wasn't just pocket change. I had a bigger price in mind like the remainder of the 100,000 his wife would be depositing into my account in the morning.

I eased down on top of him and started to grind slowly. He stopped my movements and held me tightly around the waist. It took some time getting used to his hard round stomach that made him look nine months pregnant. I needed to speed up the process because I was over it. Not to mention, it was a lot of work trying to keep his four inches inside of me. For some reason he bought a Magnum XL, which hung loosely from his child-like dick. He could've folded that thing up four times and it still would have been too big. I was happy that I worked out so much because dealing with his fat ass was definitely a struggle. The ones with the wack sex game were always killed immediately. If I couldn't get what I needed, I had no reason to prolong the inevitable.

"Baby, I wanna try something new with you. I read about it in the magazine," I said to him.

"Now, I'm not with none of the funny shit. You can do whatever but don't go anywhere near my ass," he responded anxiously.

I pulled his satin tie from around his neck and placed it over his eyes. I knew his sex would be shit when he didn't bother to fully undress. He smiled when I placed soft kisses on his lips.

"I promise this won't hurt at all. In fact, it will be over so soon, you won't know what hit you."

I leaned down and placed my hands under the pillow. I bounced up and down on his lap causing heavy moans to escape his lips. His thigh muscles tightened underneath me and I knew that it was now or never. He grabbed my hips and tried to give it to me roughly. I swear I wanted to laugh out loud at his sorry ass, kiddy fuck game.

Just when his mouth flew open to moan, I sat up and quickly placed the gun along with the silencer inside of it. Before he had time to think about what was happening, I pulled the trigger twice and watched as his brains flew against the wall. His body twitched several times and then it was over.

The smell of his blood and death mixed together immediately assaulted my nostrils. My stomach churned and I couldn't stop myself from releasing the cheap ass Red Lobster dinner that he'd just bought me prior to bringing me to this cheap ass motel. I'd never thrown up before and that fact solidified my reasoning for getting out of this game. Lady was just gonna have to understand that this hustle was over with. This life was no longer one that I wanted to live. After I handled my business with Dyson LaRue, I would become a changed woman, one who'd do normal things like bake cookies and shit.

I knew that he was far too big for me to drag his body to the tub so I had to do everything on the bed. After cleaning up my vomit, I stripped him down of his clothes, emptied his pockets except for his ID and clipped his finger nails. I grabbed a few bowls and poured bleach into them. I then soaked his hands in each one. Next, I reached in my bag for the clippers and removed all of his pubic hair. The saggy condom was placed into a container and I set it in my bag. I then poured the rest of the bleach all over the bed and then wiped the room down of any of my prints.

I thought about setting the place on fire as I left, but didn't want to bring any extra heat. After adjusting my wig, I put my sunglasses on my face, and walked out of the room into the parking lot. I looked both ways making sure that no one was watching me.

The screeching sound of tires startled me and I jumped in the grass just before a car almost hit me. I raised my head to see the back of a very familiar silver Mercedes; one that almost ran me over leaving Lady's house. It quickly turned the corner and disappeared. I stood up, dusted the dirt off my clothes, and limped back to my trunk. I desperately wanted to get inside before the car came back. I knew that incident was no coincidence. Someone was trying to kill me.

When I started the truck, my phone vibrated, scaring me even further. I was on edge as I looked at the phone and saw that it was Jamison calling. Looking at my truck's clock, it was after two in the morning so I knew he wasn't pleased.

"Hey baby, I was running late in the office, but I'm on my way now." I tried to hide my trembling voice.

"You just don't fucking get it, do you? I'll show yo ass better than I can tell you though. No more of Jamison being nice with your trifling ass," he said then hung up.

I looked at the phone in shock. I didn't think the night could get any worse until a new text message popped up. My hands shook as I looked at a picture with me and the man I'd just killed.

Chapter 6

I thought back to Lady's warning and the incident in the parking lot as I stood in the mirror applying makeup. I tried to push the bullshit from my mind and admired my look for the night. I rocked a deep red smoky eye since it was dark, seductive and would cause attention to my eyes. I painted my lips delicately with a cranberry, glossed tint.

My body adorned the perfect white goddess Gucci dress with a huge split up both sides that made my soft thighs look even more inviting. The $1,400.00 pair of studded Pigalle Christian Louboutin heels I wore were bought with Chauntelle's advance money. Shoes were something I normally splurged on with my money.

I readjusted my bra and allowed my breasts to spill from the top of my dress. I pinched my nipples to make them appear hardened. I then sprayed my favorite Tom Ford perfume in all the necessary places and smiled at my reflection.

"I swear, when your ass look like that it makes me forget how mad you make me most times," Jamison said.

He licked his lips and swiped his hand across the top of his head. He was aroused and his erection poked out of his jogging pants. My heart skipped a beat and I remembered why I'd fallen in love with him so many years ago. He was sexy as hell!

He wasn't home when I finally made it in last night. I woke the twins up to ask them if they knew where he went, but they had no information for me. I called his cell all night but he wouldn't answer. I didn't bother to ask him where he'd been when he finally showed up around six a.m., but a funny feeling in my stomach told me that he was possibly seeing someone else. That bitch was in for a rude awakening if she assumed it would be easy to take him from me though.

"You like what you see?" I asked, placing my hands on my hips. I shifted my weight to one leg and stood as if to say, 'Yes I'm working with something major between these thighs.'

Jamison walked into the bathroom and killed the space we had between us. He grabbed me around my waist with his right hand and used his left hand to grip my ass. I kissed him on his lips and he pushed his tongue inside of my mouth. He broke our kiss and stared in my eyes.

"I love you so much. I'm sick of arguing with you. I'm sick of you not being there when I need you," he said, pushing my dress to the side.

His fingers caressed my thighs so tenderly; I closed my eyes and was lost in his touch. As soon as his fingers discovered how wet I was, his desire intensified.

"I don't like when you don't wear panties, it's kind of slutty."

His mouth was all over my body. I couldn't even keep up with the fast movements of his tongue as he expertly licked on any open spot on my chest and neck.

"Maybe I'm a slutty girl," I said between shallow breaths.

Jamison was slowing down the program for me to leave on time. I needed to get out of there, but he was making me horny.

"Baby, I really have to go. We gotta wait on this," I managed to protest.

I tried to stop him, but I was too slow for his swift movements. Jamison had me in the air with my legs wrapped around his waist in a matter of seconds. He pushed my back up against the wall and inserted himself inside of me.

He drilled, I moaned. He grinded, I groaned. The sex between us was always amazing; I never had a complaint about that. It was how he made a living that I had a problem with. He was okay with having a mediocre, middle class life but I wanted more. I was tired of having to hide my fortune in a secret account, pulling a few hundred here and there. I was ready to splurge full time.

"You have to learn to let me be the man in this relationship," he said between thrusts.

"Yes, I will. I swear I will."

He nibbled my bottom lip softly. His gaze into my eyes showed me how much pain I was causing him. I felt guilty as hell.

"You fucking around on me?" he asked

I wished that I could tell him the truth, but it was ugly, and what Jamison needed was a lie covered in a beautiful moment.

"No, I never have," I whispered.

He pulled my lip towards him as he smiled. He needed his woman's reassurance, all men did. It was their weakness whether they knew it or not.

"I'm about to make you cum, baby."

His voice still held a great deal of force behind it, but his eyes were now calm and gentle. We held onto each other tightly and allowed nature to do its thing with us. His back locked tight; I dug my nails into it and relaxed. I exhaled through my tremors and covered him with my orgasm.

He sat me on the edge of the tub and pushed my hair behind my ear. His soft kisses covered my face and gave me the extra push I needed to go through with the Dyson LaRue situation. I wanted Jamison to remain in my life and getting rid of Dyson would ensure we were set for life.

"These shoes are sexy as hell. Are they new?" Jamison asked, while massaging my legs. "Wait…are those red bottoms? When the hell did you buy those?"

"I didn't buy them. I umm got these from Tayla the other day. She barely wore them so I took them from her."

I don't know where that lie came from but I was with my friend Tayla when I bought them so it kind of worked. Jamison would never understand that I paid so much for a pair of shoes, not on our fixed income of comfortable not flashy.

"Damn, Tayla got it like that, huh? Who is she sleeping with these days?"

I shook my head. "She's so into church these days, I doubt if she's dating right now."

"I'm telling you baby, soon I'm gonna be able to buy shoes like these for the woman I love all the time, and I won't need a connection. This book gone blow up and we'll have money coming out the ass," he replied.

His damn talk about writing that book became an instant mood killer for me. I pushed his hands from my legs and stood up.

"Jamison, let's not do this tonight. I need to freshen up real quick so I can get ready to go."

Taking the hint, he turned on the shower and hopped in.

"Give me fifteen minutes and I'll be ready. Where are we going tonight?"

"We? What do you mean, where are *we* going tonight, Jamison?" I stared at him through the glass door.

"I figured you always partying so I may as well join you tonight and this way we can get some time away from the kids. I'm tired of sitting in here alone," Jamison said as he lathered his body with soap.

"I do want to spend alone time with you baby, but I promised Tayla I would hang out with her tonight. She's getting over a real bad break up and need some girlie support." I scrambled to think up lies.

I'd already made plans to attend an exclusive fight party Dyson was having. I wasn't on the guest list, but I knew there wasn't a man alive who could turn me down when I looked and felt this good.

"I don't want to be all up in y'all mix. You two can do your thang and then we can hook up on the dance floor. It's been years since we hit the clubs, got drunk and had wild, insane sex."

He started practicing his dance moves in the shower and had the situation not been so serious for me, I probably would've laughed, but I was freaking out inside. I needed to take this opportunity and somehow squeeze my way into the eyes of Dyson LaRue. I had to think of a fast way to diffuse the situation.

"What about the girls? There's no way we can find a baby sitter this late. Why don't we just make plans to go out tomorrow? I don't want Tayla to think I'm flaking out on her, she needs me right now, and her latest break-up was kind of rough."

"They're seventeen, they don't need a sitter. But if it'll make you feel any better, I'll call my mother to come over," he said, stepping out of the shower completely naked.

I swallowed hard as the water glistened across his body. Even in a soft state, he was a hell of a lot bigger than the average man. I needed my ass kicked for not appreciating all he had to offer, but money needed to be made. I didn't sleep with other men because I wanted to; I did it because it was my job to make them feel good right before I snatched their lives away.

"Your mother? Oh hell no! I'm not having some drunk inside my house. Besides, she doesn't like me, and I don't like her. She hasn't been around all this time, so there's no need to call her now."

"Look, calm down Mykah. I was just making a suggestion since you're insisting that they need a babysitter. The girls are old enough to take care of themselves. If I didn't know any better, I would think you're up to something else other than hanging with Tayla."

"No, that's not it at all. I just promised Tayla, that's all."

"If she's your true friend then she would understand that you also need to spend some time with your man," he replied, walking out of the bathroom, and sitting on our bed.

Jamison leaned over and cut the fan on. He never dried off with a towel because it irritated his Eczema too bad. He took his time and massaged himself with Vaseline as the fan dried his body. He already had his outfit laid out on the bed. There seemed to be no way that I could talk him out of going with me. I would have to go to extreme measures in order to make the night a successful one.

"You right, Jamison. I'll call Tayla and reschedule. Tonight will be for you and I only." Fuck! I would have to cancel my real plans and also make a fool out of myself by calling Tayla and fake canceling our plans that were never set up. She would catch on quick though and hopefully not blow up my spot. I'd used her on more than one occasion as a valid alibi.

"I'm glad you see it my way. We're gonna have a good time tonight and get our groove back."

I laughed with him real plastic-like, but my mind was still scrambling on ways to get out of this mess. I needed to strike this oil while I could. There was no guarantee I would be able to get Lady to hook me up like that again with information.

"Baby, you want me to get you a drink while you get dressed?" I asked him sweetly.

"Yeah. I just want a lil' buzz, not get knocked on my ass," Jamison yelled, as I was already on my way out of the room, headed to the bar downstairs.

I made a quick detour to the guest bathroom and opened the medicine cabinet. I was happy to see Jamison's mother's medication was still inside of it. She had surgery a few months ago on her back and was recuperating at our house. As much as I hated having her in my home, Jamison insisted that it would be good for everyone. I resented him for it at the time. But now I was more than happy as I grabbed her leftover muscle relaxers and the Oxycontin. I figured two of them a piece wouldn't kill him, but they would knock him out strong.

I went to the bar and poured his drink halfway. I crunched up the pills and then dropped them into the glass, quickly filling the drink to the brim. I shook it slowly to allow the pills to dissolve fully.

"What are you doing?"

I jumped in surprise. I hadn't heard anyone enter the room and wasn't sure how much was seen.

"What were you doing to my daddy's drink?" Malia asked again with more attitude than a seventeen-year-old should have towards their parent.

"I'm not doing anything to his drink, not that it's any of your business. Don't you think you should be in bed by now like most kids?"

Malia rolled her scrawny neck at me and sucked her teeth. She'd just left the salon earlier that day and had bangs cut into her hair. Surprisingly, she even had the same golden highlights that I had. It was like looking at my own reflection standing in front of me, which was odd since I knew she didn't care for me these days.

"It's Saturday, and I'm not a little kid, nor am I sleepy. Shouldn't you be ready for bed or will you be on the couch again tonight?"

I was two seconds from knocking her little fast ass on her back. Her arms were folded defiantly across her chest as she gave me a piercing look that resembled mine. It was a weird feeling but it was almost as if she wanted to be me.

"Look, Malia, I don't know what your problem is, but you're over stepping a line and it's about to get you seriously hurt. You better march your lil' ass up those steps and get in the bed before you see a side of me that's reserved for my enemies," I said through clenched teeth.

"I saw what you did and I'm telling my daddy you did something to his drink," she said, spinning around to tackle the stairs.

I grabbed her shirt and pulled her back towards me. I cursed as the drink spilled down my hand and just missed my brand new shoes. She was lucky as hell that didn't happen.

"Listen, you don't know what the fuck I did, so mind your business. I'm not sure what your father told you, but whatever you're thinking about me isn't right. Men will say anything to bend things their way. Don't be a fool and fall for their lies," I spoke firmly.

"My daddy ain't that kind of man. Hell, if you were half of the woman that you should be, you would be making him happy," she said defiantly.

I couldn't stop my free hand from reaching back and coming down hard on her face. She looked at me in surprise before bawling into tears. They spilled down her cheek and I instantly felt bad. Somehow I'd lost a connection with my daughters and my husband. I was no different than a hustler who provided for his family, but was too busy making money to appreciate it with them.

"I'm sorry, Malia. I love you, your sister and daddy, too. We'll always be a family. I work late nights so I'll be here to see you off to school and when you get home from school on most days. I take pictures and that causes me to be out late sometimes, but I'd rather be at home with you all, trust me. Now go to bed. I promise to come and kiss you goodnight like I used to as soon as I give your father his drink."

Malia looked at the drink and then back at me apprehensively. She'd stop crying and the hurt in her eyes were now filled with hate. Her obsession with Jamison was becoming a bit much for me, especially since she now saw me as an enemy. After all the sacrifice I've given just to make sure she had the latest and trendiest of any clothing item, shoes or technology and she hated me. The thought of that rocked me to my core.

"I'm too old for you to kiss me goodnight or read a damn bedtime story. You missed that time a few years back when you were so called taking pictures in the club," she replied.

"I think you better get out of my face before something bad happens."

"Oh, something bad is going to happen. Trust me. I'm just waiting for my father to be a real man and tell you what's up."

I wanted to snap her damn neck in two, but I gave her another smile and nudged her towards the steps. I walked behind Malia and watched as she purposely stomped up each one. When she got to her bedroom she stopped and looked at me and then back at the drink. I could tell that she still felt some type of way.

After she slammed her door, I walked towards my room shaking my head. She reminded me a lot of myself when I was her age, too much attitude. Not only was I really starting to slip, since I didn't hear a seventeen-year-old sneak up on me, but I needed to come up with some type of lie just in case Malia decided to run her mouth. That type of shit could ruin everything.

"Damn, baby, what took you so long? I thought you forgot about me," Jamison asked as he walked out of the bedroom.

I handed him the rum and coke and watched as he downed every last drop. He licked his lips and pulled me in for a kiss. We stood there in a deep embrace before I pulled away from him and answered his question.

"I was talking to Malia. She had a few issues that she needed to discuss. Go ahead and watch the game on the couch and let me get a little alone time with the girls before we leave."

I kissed him again for reassurance. Jamison nodded his head and walked down the steps as I walked in the girls' room to let Malia know she needed to watch her damn mouth. We actually needed to get some things straight about what she'd seen. Oddly, her eyes were closed, pretending to be asleep. How was she just raising hell one minute and then knocked out the next? Jasmine was already in a deep sleep and snoring loudly. I kissed Jasmine on the cheek and walked back towards the door.

I closed their door and went to my bathroom to freshen up a little more and to give the drink some time to work its way into Jamison's system. I was still a bit nervous about going to Dyson's club, so I grabbed my phone just to check over his file one more time. More than likely there would be metal detectors so bringing my gun wouldn't be an option. However, I had a fresh razor blade in my purse just in case something popped off.

I glanced at the time and saw that twenty minutes had passed and hopefully Jamison would already be knocked out. I tiptoed through the halls past the girls' room and walked down the steps slowly. When I hit the bottom one and heard Jamison snoring on the couch, I sent up a silent 'Thank You' to God. The drink had really done a number on him and I almost felt bad for spiking it. I hoped my means would justify the end. I kissed him and grabbed my keys from the table quickly. I opened the door and prayed the alarm's chime wouldn't wake him up.

I stopped momentarily as he moved but it was only to get in a more comfortable position. I opened the door and sprinted like Allyson Felix toward my truck. I was on a mission and nothing would stop it.

Chapter 7

There was nothing fancy about the spot where, Dyson LaRue held his little after hour affairs, at least not from the outside. It was in an old office building turned into one huge loft on Washington Avenue in the heart of downtown St. Louis. There were no lights and no awning that would draw attention to it. It was hidden in plain sight. It sat in between the residential side and nightlife side of the street. As normal as it looked, I anticipated it to be hard as hell to enter without some type of divine intervention. This place was made for exclusivity.

I walked up to the entrance and pressed the button for the doorbell. This activated a video monitor that showed the face of a menacing looking bald, fat man.

"What?" he barked at me.

The fat on his neck shook through the screen. I was certain he was chosen for his position because his look alone was enough to put fear into just about anybody. However, I wasn't just anybody. If I went so far as to drug Jamison, I could easily charm my way into a club by seducing a fat bastard.

"I'm here for the party. I was told this was the location," I said seductively.

I continued to smile as he looked at me with his evil beady eyes and scanned me from head to toe through the monitor. He picked up a sheet of paper and skimmed over its contents.

"I don't see your name down," he said.

"Umm, you didn't ask me my name either."

"Exactly, now get the hell away from here."

With his last word the screen turned off and the video camera rotated back to the street. I hit the door with my hand and walked away spewing every curse word I could think of. I was so pissed that I didn't see the crowd of men in front of me before it was too late. I collided with the one in front. His foot landed firmly on mine and he caught me just before I hit the ground.

"Oh my bad, sexy, you okay?" he asked me.

"Yeah I'm fine, but you totally ruined my shoes," I said angrily in return. Several spikes had fallen off.

I forced myself from his firm grip and looked into the eyes of the man who I was searching for. *What are the fucking chances?* I thought to myself as I skimmed him from head to toe. The pictures that I had of him in my file didn't capture the full amount of sexiness surrounding the molecules that made up his 6'2 frame.

"You must forgive me and allow me to make it up to you somehow."

He smiled at me with his head cocked to the side. His skin was a bronze red that reminded me of Louisiana red clay. He had a low cut Caesar with deep waves and a rugged shadow caressed the sides of his cheeks. He'd rendered me into the state of muteness. My mind was screaming for me to say something, but I just stood there gawking at him. He was fine.

"Damn, shawty must be drunk. Its hella early and she tipping already," one of his friends behind him said.

"All that ass she working with, I need to be tipping with her," another one yelled out.

"Aye, you alright?" Dyson asked me again before turning back around to his entourage.

"She ain't saying too much of nothing, she probably on that Molly shit," another friend chimed in.

"What? I'm not on drugs. Are you crazy? I'm just in pain from you stepping on my foot."

His drug comment snapped me out of my homemade soap opera and back into reality. I looked down at my ruined shoe and wanted to cry.

"Awww, I'm sorry about that, baby girl. I just tried to keep you from falling. Trust and believe I can replace them."

He pulled a business card out of his wallet and gave it to me. He then paused for a moment making sure that I saw he carried a black American Express card. I rolled my eyes slightly as if I saw that card daily and was now bored with it. I cleared my throat and stared at him.

"I really am sorry for messing up your lil' joints. They sexy as hell on you, too," Dyson commented.

"Well, thanks, but I gotta go. This night has been a total bust and I just want to get home and sleep."

"You know someone up in there? Your man or something?" Dyson questioned while nodding his head towards the building.

"A girlfriend of mine told me about a private fight party that was going on, but unfortunately the security guard is acting like a bitch. So like I said, I'm heading home."

I walked around him and headed towards my truck with a smirk on my face and extra swinging in my hips. My shoes were ruined, but I knew my ass was still singing a sensual serenade in the dress.

"Aye, the least I can do is try and make your night a lil' better. Come on in the spot with me and I'll get you a bottle," he yelled my way.

I turned around and placed my hands on my hips. I wasn't really mad, but men like him needed a little feistiness in order to balance out their life.

"First, I'm an addict, now an alcoholic? Wow, you must be new at this? Why can't you just buy a drink? I don't need a bottle for you to try and impress me."

Dyson laughed and rubbed his hands together. The bling coming from his cufflinks was enough to blind someone. He cocked his head to the side again and bit his bottom lip. His tailored suit clung to his body as if it was hand painted on him and I wanted nothing more than to use my mouth to remove it.

"My bad, but you were looking a lil' crazy, shit. I was just playing with you but for real let me try and make your night a lil' better. Come on, as sexy as you are, you gone be my company for the evening. And trust me, I ain't new at this at all."

"Looks like you already have enough company for the evening and I don't even know you. Your ass could be the Southside rapist for all I know," I replied.

"Trust me, I don't have to take anything from a woman when it comes to sex. Besides, the rapist was caught years ago. Look, you just say the word and my boys are gone. Besides, the card I gave you tells you that my name is Dyson."

"Nice meeting you, Dyson. Tell your friends that I would like to join you for that drink and my name is umm, Mylie, my name is Mylie."

I struggled to come up with a name quickly because I had no clue that I would actually meet Dyson tonight. I had everything planned perfectly, but to bump into him this quick into the night kind of threw me off. He looked at me as if he knew I lied about my name.

"Okay, Ms. Mylie, we gone have ourselves a good time tonight. Let's go watch Mayweather do his thing."

Dyson nodded his head and his crew quickly dispersed. I was impressed that a single gesture like that seemed to be a command. He grabbed my hand and we walked back to the front door. I waited for him to press the doorbell and the sloppy top bodyguard on the other side of the monitor to appear, but Dyson just simply turned the knob and the door opened.

"I thought this was supposed to be a club," I whispered in the dark air.

I also wondered why I hadn't heard any music or any noise for that matter. Sensing my apprehension, Dyson placed his hand around my waist and drew me near him. His touch was warm, nothing like the dangerous killer he was said to be.

Keep calm, keep calm, I chanted inside.

"I love the dark vibe of the place and the rooms are all soundproof because the residential lofts are on the other side.

This way people can party all night and not a sound will come out of the building. Anything can happen here and no one on the outside will hear a thing," Dyson said as we entered an elevator.

He pushed the penthouse button and then leaned back against the wall and stared at me. I nervously slid my hair behind my ear and tried to think of something to say that would make him laugh like he did earlier.

"I'm still not one hundred percent sure you're not about to take me somewhere and do things to me. I thought I was going to a club."

He didn't give me the laugh, but he did smirk and cock his head to the side again. *Damn, he can't do anything without looking sexy as hell,* I thought as I waited on his response.

"If I was, would you be mad?" he teased.

"I guess it would depend on your performance."

"I think my reputation speaks greatly about how I perform."

"That's funny because I've never heard of you before," I responded quickly.

Playing dumb with him seemed to be my best bet. As sexy as he was, a million dollar bounty on his head was sexier. I was here on a mission only, and no matter how warm my hot pocket would get around him, I had to keep the goal in mind. Reel him and make him lose sense of reason in his pursuit to have me. I knew he was feeling me but I needed to see if he was willing to play love's favorite game of cat and mouse.

"I'm Dyson LaRue, baby. Everyone in the bi-state area either knows me or my family."

He actually looked wounded that I didn't know who he was. I was still looking for the killer in him that I'd heard so much about but for some reason I felt safe with him.

I was about to fess up and say that I'd heard of the LaRues when the elevator stopped and the doors opened to the nightclub. The sexy ambiance was breathtaking. The purple and turquoise lights illuminated the room. The waterfall in the middle of the dance floor gushed slowly down into a small stone pond that doubled as extra seating area.

The floor was marbled white tile that was perfect for the black furniture that was placed around the room along with dozens of flat screen televisions. There were also silver cages that suspended from the ceiling that housed several dancers. Their moves were more exotic synchronized performances instead of raunchy booty shakers. On the stage that sat in the corner was the jazz musician, Rhoda G, blaring out a love ballad on her saxophone.

"Beautiful, ain't it? I still get that same vibe every time these doors open," Dyson said, pulling me out of my awe stricken state.

"It's absolutely gorgeous. You come here often?" I turned to him and asked.

"Yeah, I kind of own the place so I'm here what you call often," he boasted.

He was cocky again. He rebounded quickly from my slight diss on who he was. The need to impress people was an arrogant man's demise. They were always too caught up in the hype of the moment to see what was happening.

"Really? Well in that case, I will take that bottle you offered me. I worked really hard for these shoes and now they're ruined. I'm crushed, so I will need something strong to put me to sleep tonight," I whispered in his ear.

"I'll make sure I keep that in mind," he said. The rooster stroll he put on as we walked into the VIP section made me chuckle inside. It was obvious that he was the king in his castle as everyone broke their necks to speak to him or at the least give him some dap.

We sat across from each other on the plush couches. I crossed my legs slowly and gave him a smile. Since I was without panties, I knew he got a glimpse of the kitty, but tonight would not be his lucky night. I didn't operate that way. I first needed his vulnerability and that would take some time.

No sooner than we sat down, a waitress came over with a huge bucket full of Ciroc vodka and a tray of food. I was impressed by the power that he held.

"You see what you like, Mylie? If not, I can make sure that your every need is supplied."

"This is more than enough and as far as my needs, why don't you surprise me. Just make sure it's good and sweet."

We stared at each other hard. Almost as similar as the stare down that I had with his wife Chauntelle, but this one was sexual in nature and neither of us wanted to back down. I hated his wife immediately, but I didn't hate him at all; I actually wanted to get to know him better.

He winked at me before looking away to mix our drinks. After mixing up what looked to be like one potent concoction, he raised his glass for mine to meet his.

"To new friends, supplied needs, and what I assume, based on your behavior tonight, to be one hell of a ride," he toasted and then immediately threw his drink back in one gulp.

Not one to be outdone, I stared at him and threw mine back also. I felt warm as soon as the contents hit my body. I wasn't really a big time drinker, but I appreciated a taste every now and then. I handed him my glass, looked down at my shoe and back up at him. He laughed and poured me another glass.

"I told you, I can replace those shoes. But you better slow your roll on this drink. It's stronger than you think. You may be trying to chew off more than you can swallow."

I took the glass and drunk mine quickly again, wiped the corners of my mouth and smirked at him. I leaned in closer so that he could stare at the crease in my breasts while I spoke to him.

"I thought the saying was bite off more than you can chew? But believe me, if I was chewing anything, I could definitely swallow it all."

I didn't give him time to respond because the music switched to a DJ and Beyonce's, *Partition*, blared through the speakers. I had no choice but to dance as the bass in the song and the alcohol took over my body. He sat back and watched my little pre-show, and from the huge smile on his face, I knew he was enjoying every second of it.

However, that was short lived when the ugly, fat security guard pushed his way through the crowd, and pulled Dyson's attention away by whispering something in his ear. Dyson's eyes turned cold and heartless. For the first time that night, I saw the face of the most feared man in St. Louis.

He didn't look my way as he jumped up and ran to a door in the back of the club. I didn't really think that much of it until I noticed several men with solid black suits on move to the same door. Some major shit was going down.

Chapter 8

I fought my way through the crowd, pushed opened the door that I saw the crew hurry out of, and was immediately hit with pitch black darkness. I waited against the wall until my eyes adjusted to the situation before I removed my shoes and tiptoed down the hallway. I attempted to twist the knob on every door I came in contact with but they were all locked.

I'd just gotten past the last door, before I hit the next hallway, and it opened. The cigar smoke from the room escaped into the thickness of the air and I tried my hardest not to cough as it assaulted my nose. I hid back against the wall until I heard the scuffle of feet walking back towards the nightclub's door. I slightly stuck my head around the corner and looked through the crack in the door that was left open.

There was a crowd of people gathered around a man who sat on the floor bleeding. He was naked. His hands and feet were tied. Dyson stood in front of him talking but I couldn't make out any words.

"What the fuck you doing back here?" a loud voice blared from behind me.

Startled, I turned around only to be face to face with my worst nightmare, the scary fat body guard. His arms were folded across his chest. His veins pumped through his skin reminding me of slithering snakes.

"I was looking for a bathroom. I don't feel well," I responded while backing into the hallway to remove myself from his immediate reach if things went ugly.

"Ain't no fuckin' bathroom back here and you damn sure ain't looking for it."

Thank God the loud commotion caused a few people to pile out of the room. Among them was Dyson and Lady, who I was shocked to see. They both reached out to me at the same time to see what was going on.

"I found her snooping around back here. She say she looking for a bathroom," the bodyguard spewed with acid dripped words.

"I don't feel good. I just need to freshen up a lil bit," I said to Dyson and waved my hand as if I needed air.

"You shouldn't be back here. Didn't you see all the big ass bathroom signs inside of the club?" he asked me angrily.

"I hadn't noticed them. I saw you walk out here, so I assumed the bathroom was this way. You were right about them drinks," I replied.

I looked up at him but the glare in his eyes caused me to look away. He was pissed and that made me nervous. I glanced at Lady. She shook her head back and forth with a, 'I told you so', look on her face.

"Are you lying to me because I don't like liars?" Dyson asked.

"I swear I was just looking for a bathroom."

"You want me to toss her ass, bruh?" the bodyguard asked him.

Dyson stared into my eyes before looking back in the room with the bleeding guy on the floor. I turned to look too. He looked like he was on the brink of death with all the blood that surrounded him. Surprisingly, when he looked up at me I realized he was Lady's grandson, Rick the one with the drug problem. We use to hang out together when we were little when he was a heavy hitter in the drug game. His flashy lifestyle then was the opening act for his cliché drug dealer turned junky life. He now cleaned the bathrooms at one of the LaRues Laundromats. My heart tugged to see him like that.

"Is he okay?" I asked Dyson.

"You shouldn't have come back here," he replied before turning to his bodyguard. "Get her out of here man, I don't know what she saw."

"Wait, what? I didn't see anything at all. I'm just looking for the bathroom," I responded in panic mode.

"You bet not put yo' damn hands on that girl, boy," Lady spoke up as she hobbled on her cane moving closer to me.

She was dressed in white skinny jeans, red loafers and a blue and white buttoned up sleeve shirt. She wore a pair of red Prada frames that weren't as dark as her normal shades, but still had a heavy cherry tint on them. I'd never been so happy to see her crooked smile and wig in all my life. I felt ambushed by Dyson and his housedog.

"No offense, Lady, but you need to be worrying about the motherfucker in there on the floor and how the fuck you gone come up with the money he stole," the bodyguard said to her.

"I been wipin' this lil' girl ass since before yo' ass could pee straight. If you put a single finger on her I'll cut them bitches off, batter 'em up and feed them to you myself," Lady said roughly.

"Man, fuck what this old bitch talking about, Dyson. You know what your Pops said to do. I would hate to be the man to disobey that shit," the bodyguard attempted to whisper in Dyson's ear.

"Dyson, unless you want to be a pallbearer at that boy's funeral, you'll tell yo' pit bull to sit. The way this girl sweatin' and jumpin' up and down, she either gone piss all over yo' expensive floor or pass the fuck out. Last thing you need is the police in here. Wouldn't Daddy Dearest be more pissed about that?"

"Right, I swear I can't hold it much longer," I said while bouncing around.

I didn't really have to pee, but if Lady threw the bone out there I was sure going to assist in it being caught. Dyson's face softened a little bit when he heard Lady speak up for me.

"This yo' peoples, Lady?" he asked her.

"Yeah, she real good peoples, too. I reckon I find myself fond of her lil' high-strung ass," she replied.

"I don't give a damn if she know the Pope, I don't trust her ass, Dice," the bodyguard said.

"She ain't gotta know the Pope when she know a boss bitch like myself. Don't act like I ain't wipe yo' rotten ass, too, Kip," Lady said to the bodyguard.

Dyson appeared to be taking what Kip said into consideration. I realized that he and Dyson were close enough for him to be a for real problem for me. I wanted to smack his damn meaty head on the floor, but I was too busy holding my breath as I waited for Dyson to speak next.

"Yo', why you ain't tell me you know Lady?" he asked me with a huge smile on his face.

"I didn't know you knew her, but of course everybody does know her," I responded with a fake laugh.

I was relieved that apparently Lady's words held more weight with Dyson than Kip's. The mood had lightened but Kip's chest was swollen with anger.

"If you know Lady then you alright with me. It seems like she the fairy Godmother tonight, saving lives and shit," he said.

For the first time I noticed that he held a whip in his hand. Dyson must have beaten Lady's grandson with it, which would explain why he was bleeding so badly.

"That's typical Lady, always trying to assist those in need," I said to him.

"Lady, you can collect your property and take it out the back door. Come see me in the morning to handle that business. And the rest of y'all clean that mess up while I finish enjoying my evening," Dyson ordered.

I noted how everyone moved into action as soon as he spoke, even Lady seemed to stand up straight and move faster. We walked back down to the end of the hallway where the door was. I made sure to roll my eyes extra hard at the gorilla of a bodyguard.

Dyson opened the door to the club and we stepped back inside. Lady moved to my side and whispered in my ear over the loud music.

"You look real sloppy tonight. Done got me involved in yo' mess. I swear if you get us wrapped up in some shit, the devil will run from hell after I'm done wit' yo' ass. Get yo' shit together. "

I nodded my head to let her know that I understood. She threw a final glance my way then fell back behind us. Now that I was out of trouble, her number one concern was her grandson.

The thickness of the crowd caused a separation between Dyson and me. I turned around trying to find him, when my eyes landed on my best friend, Tayla, dancing with a man in the corner. He was bald and sort of on the fat side. From the tailored suit he wore, I could tell that money flowed freely in his pockets. I was dying to know if this was the man who'd been keeping her under wraps. I changed my paths and made my way towards them.

What in the hell was Tayla doing in Dyson's spot? I wondered. *When I called her earlier today she told me that she would be at some church revival.*

I'd almost reached Tayla when the music switched from mellow to raunchy hip-hop and the crowd went nuts. I had to block flinging bodies left and right just to make it safely across the floor. I looked for Tayla again but she was gone and there was another woman standing where I thought she was. The woman had on a waitress uniform and was serving the man a drink. Several other waitresses walked over to him to make sure that he was okay. Whoever he was, it seemed that he held just as much power as Dyson did. I shook my head and laughed at myself for thinking I saw Tayla. Those drinks had really started to take effect on me. I guess I just missed spending time with her. She'd really been off on her own lately. I turned back around and bumped into Dyson's solid chest for the second time that night.

"We really have to stop doing all this bumping with no grinding," he said to me.

"Who said we would ever get to the grinding part?" I shot back.

"Your body said it when you were dancing for me. Your mouth didn't have to say anything."

"This same body that you were about to toss out in the trash?"

"Man, you just ran up on me at a bad time. I would never toss you out," he replied as smooth as ever.

I swallowed the saliva that gathered in my mouth and tried desperately to think of something other than having sex with him right on the spot.

"I'm tired. Why don't you give me your number? I'm going to head home."

"Alright Ms. Mylie, put your math in my phone so I can make sure to stay in touch."

"My math?"

He laughed at me and explained that my math was actually my phone number. We exchanged information and we both just stood there. It was obvious that neither of us wanted to leave, but I was well aware that I needed to go.

"It was nice meeting you, Dyson. I look forward to speaking with you again."

"Well I got you locked in," he said with a smile on his face.

I quickly switched away from him and stopped in the bathroom just to splash some water on my face. I had enough excitement for the night and I knew when to draw the white flag and surrender. I looked up in the mirror and saw Chauntelle's gray eyes. She was standing directly behind me.

"Wha-what are you doing here?" I asked her as I stammered over my words.

I didn't know who was creepier, her or that bodyguard, but I wanted nothing to do with either one of them.

"I could ask you the same thing since you're hugged all up and dancing with my husband. You sure don't look like you're about to murder him to me," she responded with attitude.

I grabbed her arm and dragged her into the open stall. She fought a little but still came along with me. She reeked of alcohol but her makeup was still on point and not a single hair on her head was out of place.

"Look, girl, keep your damn voice down saying shit like that. I said I would handle it and I will. I don't move on your time, remember?" I hissed at her through clinched teeth.

"I have shit that I need to do with that money from that life insurance policy so speed up your process or you'll be the one lying in dirt," Chauntelle threatened as she wrestled her slender arm from my grasp.

"I'll do it, but I won't get caught because you want me to rush. So, fall back and don't contact me until I contact you, Chauntelle. You ain't the only one invested in this shit. I had to drug my damn husband just to get out the house tonight."

"That's your damn problem, not mine. Don't slip up, Mykah. I have my new life planned in a timely manner and I don't like when people don't keep their word."

I was tired of her idle threats. Whether she was an evil bitch or not didn't matter to me because I was nobody's punk. My nerves were already amped from the alcohol and it seemed these exchanges between us were about to get live.

"Don't keep threatening me. If your bark had just a little bit of bite in it, you would've gotten rid of your husband yourself."

"Look, you just play your role as a hired hand. Don't let those new shoes make you lose sight of who holds the power. I want him dead and damn-it that shit better happen soon."

She rolled her eyes at me one final time and exited the stall and bathroom in two long strides. Kip ran to her side and helped her walk through the crowd. I noticed his hand linger on her ass as he sat her down on the couch gently. The two of them looked to be a lot closer than they should to me. I continued to stare at them until he looked up and glared at me. I shook off the tingle of fear that shot threw me and got the hell out of there.

Chapter 9

"Wait a minute. Let me get this straight, you fucking drugged, Jamison!" Tayla screamed across the room at me.

I slowed down the speed on the treadmill to a cool down mode. I grabbed my bottle of water and took a very long swig from it as I tried to slow my heart rate. I spent the past hour trying to run off some of the stress that I felt lately

"Don't you dare fucking get quiet on me now. I can't believe this shit. I swear I can't. You need to get your ass into church immediately because you're so heading to hell. I tell you that much."

I winced at the harsh language she used because she recently gave up cursing. She claimed it was an addiction. Tayla, was what some would consider a professional curser. Her family was full of people who you would rather fight with your fist than go word to word arguing with. She could tear a person to shreds with a few of her famous tongue-lashings, but she was also the sweetest person I knew and that's why I loved her so much.

Even though we talked on the phone as much as possible I never discussed business over the phone with her. So, I spent the last hour catching Tayla up to speed with the Dyson and Chauntelle situation. Lady had warned me to never tell anyone about what I had going on, but I couldn't keep a lie from Tayla. We'd grown up from the cradle together and she knew everything about me. Besides, I knew she would never cross nor judge me. She hadn't really seemed too concerned with the story until I said that I had to drug my husband. That caused her to pay attention immediately and from the deep frown that set in her face, she wasn't happy about it.

"I know Tayla, that was foul as hell of me, but he didn't leave me much of a choice. He was so excited to go out and kick it. What else could I do?"

"You know I've never questioned you about anything you do. While I wouldn't do it, I support you because you're closer to me than my own family and they say you can't choose your family. You need to repent and stop this damn foolishness immediately," she responded with her chubby hands outstretched to the heavens.

Tayla was what most people considered fat, but she had one of the most beautiful faces I'd ever seen. Her nose was a tiny little thing in the middle of two plump cheeks. Her jet black hair was in a short, pixie cut like the one Rihanna rocked periodically and framed her face perfectly.

"I'm not going to church, Tayla. I wish you'd stop all of this nonsense about what your Pastor said. You act like you worship the dude or something." I stepped off of the treadmill and plopped down in my chair.

"You need to stop the bullshit. How can you sit there and call talking about God some nonsense because you get a kick out of killing people?" she asked me with wide eyes.

Tayla had recently joined a church about a year ago. Apparently her new boo had turned her onto it and she seemed to be brainwashed by their pastor if you asked me. The sun apparently rose, set and was created in the crack of his ass. Every other sentence had some sort of church reference in it. Truthfully, the shit irked the hell out of me. However, her new mystery man had Tayla believing they should repent for their secret affair, so that's what she did. I tried to get her to bring him around for drinks so I could see if he was a cult leader, but she said he was too private of a person for that. Nevertheless, Tayla was in church every moment when she wasn't at home waiting on another woman's husband.

I was happy that she was getting some peace in her life though. But if she tried to force me to go to church one more time, I was going to add her to my, *be killed* list.

"I'm sorry, I'm not trying to make a fool out of you nor your so called God. I just need to take this last assignment so my family can be set."

"Y'all ain't hurting for money, Mykah! You can tell Jamison that shit and he believe you but I know the real deal, honey."

"We could do a lot better. Remodeling the house used a lot of the money I had saved up."

I tried to reason with her, but when I saw her withdraw the emergency silver flask from her bag I knew it was no use. Drinking was also something that she quit right around the time that her new lover pushed her into the arms of the Lord. She took a swig of the patron and shook her head at me like a mother scolding a stubborn child.

"Got damn-it, I been doing good! No cussing and no drinking for weeks now. I come around your ass for five minutes and I'm fucking doing both. I need to repent and your ass needs to do the same. God will forgive you, He forgives everyone and everyday should be a day that you thank him for his everlasting love!" she yelled my way.

"Tayla, come on now, let's not be dramatic and start calling on the prayer warriors. I know you speeding in the fast lane on the highway to heaven and all, but I need some help over here. I feel guilty as hell."

"Your ass should feel guilty and a lot more. What you did to Jamison was dangerous. You could've killed him. We need to pray about this shit!" she continued to yell.

I felt bad enough as it was because Jamison had said very few words to me since I drugged and left him sleep on the couch. When I got back that night he was upstairs in our bed asleep. Our wedding picture sat smashed on the floor and his wedding ring was at the bottom of the toilet. I tried to explain to him that he wouldn't wake up when I shook him, but obviously Jamison didn't even want to hear it. His weeklong silent treatment was killing me.

"Well, apparently that's what I do, Tayla. I kill men for a living, remember?"

"Listen, smart ass, don't get cute with me because the house that Mykah built is starting to crumble. Jamison is a good man and any woman would be lucky to have him. I can't believe you straight drugged him to go hang out. He would never forgive you for that because that was some low shit."

"He doesn't know I drugged him, but thanks for reminding me that I'm trifling," I said with an exasperated look on my face.

I reached for her flask and took a swig or three of the liquid poison for myself. At least the alcohol would numb the realization that I had really gone too far. If my marriage fell apart and Jamison took the kids, what would serve as my purpose of doing what I did? I was strictly in this to give my family a good life.

"Hey, don't beat yourself up too much. You already know your ass was trifling. If you didn't, I sure in the hell did," Tayla said while laughing.

I smiled at her silliness and was thinking of a wise comeback when a deliveryman walked in the office. I wasn't expecting anything so I was more than curious about what he had for me. There were several small packages plus a note. I signed off on the clipboard and Tayla and I began to unravel the packages as soon as he walked back out the door.

Five boxes and they all carried five different pairs of Christian Louboutin shoes; one included the same pair I wore the night I met Dyson. I knew without reading the card he was behind this, but Tayla didn't. She snatched it from my fingertips, ripped it open and read to herself with her mouth wide open.

"Well, what does it say, fool?"

I tried to pretend like I wasn't the least bit interested, but I was. I knew how expensive those shoes were and the fact that he bought me five pair excited the hell out of me. Truth be told, it turned me on. Something like this alone made me question if Chauntelle was telling the truth about him. He'd been nothing but generous to me, well except for when he was about to have me tossed out of his club.

"It says thanks for giving him head, it was the best he ever had," Tayla stated with a voice full of suspicion.

I burst out laughing and held my side as I attempted to stop the fit of giggles that shook my entire body. Tayla thought she was slick, but I knew that she was lying just to see if I was truthful about me and Dyson.

"No it doesn't, we didn't even go that far. Good try though."

"I'm just checking, hooker, because a man doing this for some cookie he ain't even bit is just unheard of."

She laughed with me and tossed the card my way. It reeked of his cologne. The smell was beyond intoxicating. I took a deep breath and inhaled slow. That little move made me anxious to read the words that would accompany sending a piece of him to me.

I apologize for our brief meeting and departure the other night. Please enjoy a day of pampering to make up for my less than gentleman-like behavior. My driver will take you to Studio Posh for a full makeover, Frontenac Plaza to find the perfect outfit for the night and lastly to me for a gourmet dinner. Make it sexy and you'll be dessert.

Apparently the shoes were just the beginning of what would be a Cinderella day for me. Something Jamison had never done. Hell, he didn't even have the means to do it anyway. I needed a man like Dyson in my life permanently. I'd been the bread winner for too long and I was sick of it.

"You sure do seem to be swooning to me, *Mrs.* Rice," Tayla teased. "I know that look, Mykah. You really like this dude and I think you need to chill and get your focus back."

I noted the emphasis she put on the word, *Mrs.* by raising my eyebrow at her, but I didn't stop reading the instructions that Dyson had written for me to follow.

This is a lot of money he spent for real. What did you say he do again?" Tayla inquired.

"You have to promise you won't freak out," I replied slowly.

"If it ain't Jesus coming back, nothing would shock me. Spit it out."

"He's a LaRue and I'm sure you know they do it all," I said while looking over the card again.

The look on Tayla's face told me she was shocked.

"A LaRue? Are you fucking nuts? Girl, they're going to kill you and the only person who can save that ass is Jesus. I heard they're dangerous as hell, Mykah. We need to pray for your safety right now and several times of the day. You really are going to need the army of the Lord to save you."

I rolled my eyes at her worried look. Her eyes darted everywhere in the room but at me. Tayla was hiding something. I knew her like the back of my own ass. Something was going on with her.

"What the hell is wrong with you? I don't need you to remind me about nothing, I got this."

"Look, I get it's yo life and all that, but I'm just trying to save you some heartache. All this fairytale shit you feeling won't get you nothing but hurt. So fuck him, handle your business and then get the money. That's the bottom line," Tayla responded while throwing her head back to receive another quick shot.

"Wait, you were just telling me to stop doing my job and join the Christian band, now you *want* me to kill him? I'm confused."

"Look, I'm new at saving souls. Hell, I barely got my foot in the door, but I know when I smell some big time drama about to fry up. Look, take care of him before that crumbling house of yours becomes a sandcastle blown away by the wind."

I swear I tried my hardest not to laugh at her, but that horrible analogy threw me over the edge and I doubled over again. She sounded like a drunk aunt giving out unsolicited advice.

"You just thought you spit some deep shit right there," I managed to get out through catching my breath.

"Laugh now but when Jamison jets off into the sunset with another chick and your kids, you'll be crying. I just have a bad feeling about this, Mykah. I can't shake it either. Don't you ever get tired of all that sneaking and the lying?"

The serious look Tayla wore on her face stopped my laughter immediately. She sat back in the chair looking like she was about to puke. She attempted to remove the beads of sweat that seemed to run down the side of her face.

"Tayla, what's up with you girl? Why you sweating so bad, you okay?"

I ran to her side and attempted to fan her with the card that I couldn't seem to part with. She pushed me off and stood back up.

"Ain't nothing wrong with me. I've been drinking and it's starting to kick in," she responded defensively and a little too agitated for my liking.

Something was definitely going on with her and for some reason she didn't want to include me in on whatever it was. She was too busy worrying about my business at the moment.

"Okay, if you say so but just know that I know when you trying to hide something," I told her.

"Look, don't worry about me. You need to be worried how the hell Dyson know where your place of business is when you gave him a fake name. You so caught up on them damn shoes that you can't see that he one step ahead of you. He knows who you are."

Tayla made a good point that I hadn't even thought about. As far as Dyson was concerned, he thought my name was Miley. How could he have known the truth? I thought back to that night and that reminded me I'd seen Tayla and some mystery man in there.

"Speaking of people being a step ahead of someone, I saw you at Dyson's club that night and it totally slipped my mind. How you know about it?" I asked her.

"What? You, umm, you didn't see me at Dyson's club. I don't even know where it is," she stammered.

"You think I don't know what you look like? We've been friends since birth. I could identify you even if I was blind so why lie?"

"Look bitch, I said you didn't see me there so get off my case and figure out how Dyson knows who the hell you are. You don't think that's funny or do you not give a damn because of some overpriced ass shoes?" she stated angrily.

"You sound a lil' jealous. Your new man broke or something? You can have a pair of the shoes if that's what you bitching about."

"Wow, so you think this is about some damn shoes? You sound like a damn fool, but deep down you know I'm right about Dyson."

She was combative which meant she was guilty. I wanted to beat the truth out of her, but now wasn't the time for me to argue with her. I had a great day ahead of me.

When my phone rang and I saw that it was Jasmine, I hit the speaker button glad for a distraction.

"Hello honey," I said.

"Hey, Ma, we're having a banquet tonight for the dancers. I heard that I might win the Shining Star award so I was hoping that you would be there tonight," she informed with excitement. "Ma, you don't understand. The Shining Star award means that I'm pretty much the best dancer on the team." Jasmine chuckled.

"Oh no, I'm sorry, baby, but I have to work tonight."

Jasmine was silent.

"I promise I'll make the next one honey. You just gotta give me more notice."

I could've sworn I heard her sniff.

"Jasmine, baby…are you crying?"

"Whatever," she said before hanging up abruptly.

I stared at the phone. I really wanted to go, but there was no way I was going to miss my date with Dyson. I just hoped that one day my daughter would understand.

"You're really turning into a horrible person, Mykah. Was your childhood that bad that it makes you turn a cold heart to everyone, even your own damn children? All this shit for money and some damn man who knows who you are…when he shouldn't?" Tayla asked.

I thought about her words for a moment and my eyes welled up with tears. I felt them trying to fall, but I pushed my thoughts of my family to the furthest spot in my mind. Back there they didn't exist and it was easier for me to handle my business.

"Goodbye,Tayla. You're more than welcome to chill here and sleep off that alcohol if you can't drive," I stated.

I chose to ignore her comments about Dyson. It hadn't crossed my mind that Dyson had obviously dug up some information about me until she said it. We'd only spoken on the phone twice since the night I met him and each time he never asked what I did for a living. As far as my family went, Tayla's opinion on that didn't matter much either.

"You know what, you right. It may be the alcohol like you said, so I'm leaving. I have to head to church and help Pastor with bible studies anyway. Call me later on and tell me how it went," she said.

"Thank you for only half way judging this situation with your newfound Christian philosophy."

"I'm going to let that slide only because I know you're blinded in ignorance by the world. Jesus can really change lives, Mykah. You just have to get to know him. Speaking of change, I really think you should call your father. If you get all that anger towards him out of your system, you'll feel a lot better."

If I wasn't already pissed at Tayla and her self-righteous ass comments, her last sentence almost made me flat line. I stared at her like she was an enemy.

"Now I know that church has you in some type of cult. You know good and damn well that me calling that man will never happen. You sound dumb as hell for even suggesting it. First Jamison, then Lady, and now you. What the hell is wrong with you people?"

"You know what, you right. I could talk until Jesus came and you still wouldn't get it. Let's just drop it."

Tayla stood and hugged me tightly. I knew that was her way of apologizing, but she held on a little longer than normal. We headed towards the door but stopped suddenly and took cover when a brick came smashing through the window, breaking the glass and sending us into a panic. Tayla screamed hysterically as I belly crawled to my desk to retrieve my nine millimeter from the bottom drawer. I was shocked when I saw that it wasn't in there. I knew I hadn't removed it. Someone was really fucking with me.

"Tayla, stop screaming and calm down. I got this," I said trying to reassure her.

The truth of the matter was that I was also trying to reassure myself. I peeked over the desk trying to see if anyone was still outside. When I didn't see anything, I stood up and walked slowly toward the brick lying on the floor. I flipped it over looking for a note, or any kind of clue as to who could have done this.

Tayla stood up, still visibly shaken. She prayed real quick and then walked towards the window.

"Mykah, where the fuck is your car and what the hell is going on?" she asked nervously.

I looked out of the broken window and saw that my vehicle was missing and the word whore was spray painted in red in its spot. It didn't seem like much evidence to go on but it let me know this was a personal vendetta for someone. Whoever that person was, pulled out of the parking lot slowly in the same silver Mercedes from the other night. Those damn tinted windows kept me from seeing anything.

All I could do was cringe. I really needed to figure out what happened to my gun and who was after me.

Chapter 10

After explaining to Tayla about the text messages I'd been receiving lately, she thought it would be best if she dropped me off at home. I declined her offer and called Dyson, telling him that someone had stolen my truck. He quickly sent a car service to pick me up and assured me that he would have everyone out searching for my ride. Even though I had a great day of being pampered at Dyson's expense, I was still mad as hell about my truck. Whoever was fucking with my life would be a done deal whenever I figured it out. I'd been so busy lately that I never even sat down to think about all the possible enemies I had.

"You look amazing," Dyson said to me as I walked into his arms for a hug.

"Thank you. You know you really didn't have to do all of this," I told him.

"I know, but I wanted to apologize for my behavior the other night and hopefully cheer you up about that shit that happened to you today. Like I told you earlier, I got everybody out looking for your truck." He handed me a glass of champagne, which I downed instantly.

"Well, thank you. I filed a police report, too. I can't tell you how much I appreciate that. You turned a horrible day into a great one."

"I'm just getting started. C'mon," he said while pulling me towards the table that sat in the middle of the floor.

The club was closed, but it would be our destination for the night. I thought it couldn't be any more perfect than when I saw it my first night, but I was wrong. Dyson had the room transformed into an imitation of what heaven would be like. White sheer fabric covered the walls and the floor had white candles and flowers spread across it. The ceiling was adorned with thousands of twinkling white lights that looked like stars. It was very romantic.

"Dyson, this is absolutely beautiful. I love this."

"I'm glad you do. I want you to be happy."

I smiled before kissing him softly on the cheek. It felt good to hear a man say that my happiness was his number one goal. Jamison never gave me that and if this was a reflection of how Dyson treated Chauntelle, she was a damn fool not to love it.

Dyson grabbed my face and kissed me softly on the lips. His tongue pushed inside of my mouth and I welcomed its taste. He then pulled me closer into his arms and inhaled deeply.

"Have a seat. Your food is right behind you."

I turned and looked at the waiters who stood patiently with our food. I hadn't even heard them walk in the room. My vision blurred and I closed my eyes to readjust my contacts. My body temperature rose to a hotter degree and a tiny drop of perspiration ran down my spine. Either Dyson's kiss had cast a spell on me or that damn champagne wasted no time with setting me off. I needed to sit before I fainted on the spot.

"This is too much. I can't believe you had food delivered, too," I said while taking my seat.

"This day is all about you. I wasn't sure what you like so I prepared chicken, seafood, pork and beef."

"Are you trying to tell me that you cooked all of this?"

"I'm not trying; I'm flat out telling you that I made all of this for you. I don't cook often but when I do, I can throw down."

Dyson pulled his chair out and took a seat across from me. The waiters almost ran towards us making sure that his food was in front of him immediately. The smirk that tugged at his lips was cocky. Dyson knew he was the man and I can't lie and say I didn't catch a vibe off his confidence.

"I'll take the seafood," I replied.

Once I made my choice, the food was placed down and the waiters magically disappeared from our presence. The huge lobster tail that sat in front of me looked succulent and juicy. I hurried to take a tiny piece trying to be cute, but as soon as it hit my tongue and melted into my taste buds I knew that I had a tough battle ahead of me. On one hand I wanted to dig into it, but I was on a date and that wouldn't be sexy.

Dyson stifled a laugh and loosened the bowtie that sat at his neck. The first three buttons on his shirt were undone and he removed his cufflinks to roll up his sleeves. He tore into his steak as if he was the only person in the room.

"Wow, here I am trying to eat cute and you're over there committing sexual assault on a dead cow."

"That's all on you. I like to eat and I like to eat well. I advise you to dig in," he managed to get out between bites.

Even when eating like a pig he was still sexy as hell to me. I couldn't find one good reason to want to kill him. Well, other than the money and my family. *Maybe I could just give it a little more time,* I told myself. I couldn't really figure out why I was hesitant about going through with it, other than the fact that I found him intriguing. I could actually see myself getting use to being with him. There was something about him that was so different from the other men in the past. He didn't seem selfish or abusive. I mean, he was a cheater, which I hated, but he didn't seem like the usual man whore. I didn't really know what the apprehension was about but I would have to worry about that later because it was now my time to kick back and enjoy what was in front of me. I took his advice and ate comfortably.

"So, what should I know about you…*Mykah*?"

I almost choked hearing him call me by my real name but I kept my poker face tight. Dyson had finished his food first and was now nursing a small glass of Hennessy no rocks and definitely no soda. I could smell the contents across the table. I really needed to get to the bottom of how much he really knew. "Well, there isn't much to know. I'm thirty-three years old and I was born and raised right here in St. Louis.

He stared at me. "Thirty-three? Wow, you look so young. You look more like eighteen. Hell, you look younger than me."

I blushed a bit. Looking into his eyes, I couldn't help but notice how sexy he looked. "Yeah, I get that a lot."

"And your body is banging. You must work out a lot. Especially those thick thighs."

"Yeah, I do. I probably should've been a personal trainer instead of a photographer. Speaking of that, how did you know my name and where I work?"

"I know everything about the people who come into my life. You didn't seem like a Mylie."

"Oh really?" I laughed then became more serious. "Dyson, I hated giving you a fake name but you can't trust people these days."

"Understood," he said looking at me sensually.

"So, how did you find out about me?"

"I had one of my boys run your license plate. I hope you and your husband don't mind me sniffing around," he stated smoothly.

I tried to hide the shocking expression on my face just in case he was looking for some sort of reaction. Shit, Tayla was right though, Dyson was definitely one step ahead of me.

"Ummm…my husband and I are currently not seeing eye to eye on a lot of things. We're only married on paper. What about you? You have any attachments?" He'd totally thrown me off guard.

I lied effortlessly. Dyson didn't need to know any of my personal information. That was one of my top rules of my business. Him getting to know the real me was something that would only confuse the situation further.

"I have a very spoiled wife that I've been separated from for about six months now. She doesn't want me, but her ass can't seem to part with the lifestyle that I've given her."

The mention of Chauntelle caused my ears to perk up to attention. I thought he would lie and tell me there wasn't a wife. I was shocked to hear they were separated though. She hadn't told me that when we first met. I wondered what other secrets her conniving ass was hiding.

"Do you think there's a chance for reconciliation?"

Chauntelle had made him out to be a monster, but I hadn't witnessed any of that so far, other than him whipping Lady's grandson Rick's ass. But I was certain there was a good reason for that as well. Normally, I was good at judging someone's character and with Dyson I felt like he was good peoples.

"Nawl, not much left to that situation. She burned bridges that could never be repaired. She crazy as fuck and hell bent on revenge because I dismissed her. Life is too short to be unhappy and we both were," he informed. "But enough about that, we're here to celebrate you tonight."

He was done with the conversation, but I wouldn't be me if I didn't keep prying. This was a part of my job in the situation.

"I appreciate that but I wanna make sure I won't have to worry about her running up on me with that loud, ghetto, 'why are you with my man' shit."

"She's too classy for that. She's more of a sneaky, underhanded type of person. I know that from personal experience."

"I'm sorry to hear that. Maybe you bumping into me and ruining my shoes was fate's way of putting something good in your life."

Dyson stood up from the table, walked over to me and grabbed my hand. I wasn't done eating and was slightly irritated that he was taking me away from the mouthwatering food without asking if I was finished. He walked me over to the VIP area with the plush couches. As soon as my body hit the pillows, I melted into them. I was tired and somewhat sleepy. The day had been a long one for me. I tried to cover the yawn that pulled at my lips, but Dyson heard it. He sat down and looked at me with an annoyed face.

"Am I boring you, Mykah?"

"No, this is all amazing. I woke up kind of early today and it's catching up with me. I swear this has nothing to do with you," I rushed to explain.

Trying to rejuvenate myself I reached for the glass of champagne that sat on the table and downed it. His staff was excellent in ensuring that everything was ready and perfect for the night.

"Oh, okay because I was going to be a little mad if you were leaving me so early. Why don't you slow up on the champagne for now? You're starting to sweat a little bit."

With Dyson issuing one command after the next, if he was guilty of anything it was being a control freak. I sat back and followed his lead. He smiled and grabbed a napkin from the table and began to gently wipe my face. His lips were so close to me, there was no way I could stop myself from kissing them. It was deep and full of raw passion.

Suddenly, I slid onto his lap and straddled him. He put his arms around my waist and I was so close to him I could feel his heart beating against my chest. I was even hotter than I was a few seconds ago. His hands were like lava touching my entire being.

"Damn, Mykah, you feel softer than I imagined you would," Dyson whispered in my left ear.

The bass of his voice boomed in my eardrum. It was a wrap. I knew right then and there I was about to give him all of me. I unbuckled his pants and ran my hand down the front of them. He was much bigger than I anticipated which was like extra icing on a cake. What person in their right mind would complain about that?

I leaned up and he slid my dress slowly over and off my body. His hands held my back firmly as he nibbled on my collarbone. The no panty thing always was a plus for eager men who needed it immediately. Dyson pushed inside of me slowly. The feeling was an indescribable one in one of the best ways possible. I moved in circular motions as I adjusted to him. He held my hips to push further inside of me. This was another odd move for me because I always made the other men use protection, but I didn't want Dyson to stop and get himself together. I don't know if it was the alcohol, but him being in me raw turned me on immensely.

Dyson pumped with excitement and the more he pounded, the wetter I became. My original plan was to ride his ass to sleep. I knew alcohol would be involved and that mixed with a powerful nut would knock any man out. It would be easy for me to kill him, but after getting a dose of what he was working with, I was going to have to sample this one more time before I put a couple of bullets in him.

"Oh my God, Dyson, I can't handle it," I moaned to him.

"Yes you can, just relax and breathe. This was special made for me. I can feel it," he replied.

Dyson was making me his bitch. That's right, he owned my ass as he flipped, dipped and dicked me down with precision. By my third orgasm I'd completely forgotten about my plan to force him into taking an eternal nap. The only thing that was getting put to sleep was me.

As I lay in his arms, eyes closed, my thoughts ran wild. I loved being in his presence. I loved the way he treated me. I loved the feel of his body. I loved everything about him. This wasn't how I normally operated but Dyson's magnetism had me gone. Hours passed and before we knew it we'd been sleeping peacefully like two lovers until someone notorious showed up.

"Look at this shit here. Dyson, get your weak ass up and meet me in the office, now!" a voice suddenly yelled out.

I wasn't sure who it was but the way Dyson tossed me to the side like a rag doll, I knew he was important. I rolled over and looked up at a very large, brown skin man who strongly resembled Dyson standing over me. He was bald on the top of his head, but still had hair on the sides, which reminded me of Uncle Phil from *Fresh Prince of Bel-Air*. He even had a huge Santa Claus shaped stomach. The menacing look on his face scared the fuck out of me. I quickly looked away from him as I scrambled to cover myself with the couch pillows we'd tossed on the floor.

Kip stood off to the side laughing as if he was at a comedy show. I swear he worked my nerves with his bad timing and I hoped Dyson was about to tell him to leave, but he stumbled over his own feet as he rushed to get dressed. The man spun around on his feet and exited the room. Within seconds, Dyson ran after him like a flunky, forgetting that I was in the room. However, Kip was fully aware, and he seemed to be more amused by the second.

"Dyson, I'm going to need a way home!" I yelled after him.

He stopped and turned to look at me awkwardly. He was obviously embarrassed that I'd witnessed him losing his cool, but shook it off quickly before barking commands again.

"Aye, turn yo' ass around so she can get herself together and then drop her off at home for me," Dyson ordered. He looked at me. "Look, I gotta go handle this shit with my pops, baby, but I promise to make it up to you." Dyson didn't even wait for a response before he disappeared.

I sucked my teeth as I attempted to cover myself and gather my clothes. I couldn't believe that Dyson had just abandoned me like that and the last person I wanted to be alone with was this big ass gorilla of a man. The way he stared at me made my body cringe.

"I don't know why you trying to hide your body, you ain't got shit I want anyway," Kip said to me. Preston will put an end to this shit here. Dyson's pop don't play," he added.

"Fuck you! Just do your job as the hired help and take me home," I returned.

I pulled my dress down over my head and rushed to put my shoes on. Kip laughed as I continued to spew curse words about the situation under my breath. I was beyond pissed.

I stormed ahead of him and pushed the back door so hard that it hit the wall loudly. As loud as it was nothing could drown out the sounds of Dyson's father berating him in his office.

"You suppose to be handling business, but yet I find you here in some pussy. I knew I shouldn't have trusted you with this. You say you want to one day run some shit, but you can't even put an end to a fucking druggie that stole from you!" Preston yelled.

I stopped in my tracks and waited on Dyson to use some sort of comeback but he didn't mutter a word. I wanted to walk in there and save him, but I had a feeling that Preston LaRue wouldn't have a problem whatsoever with killing me.

Kip and I walked in silence to the garage. I was grateful that he didn't say anything to me because I wasn't certain if I would be able to hold my tongue from going off on him. If that wasn't enough then the gun that I held in my purse would most definitely stop him if need be.

He stopped in front of a white cargo van that reminded me of the vehicles kidnappers drove in Lifetime movies. With dark tinted windows and tires that were dirty and mismatched, I looked at Kip like he was crazy.

"I'm not getting in this shit," I said to him.

He looked at me like I was the one who had a few screws loose. His nose flared up and the look in his eyes could only be described as hate.

"If yo' funky ass wanna go home, this the only way. So get in," he responded angrily.

I sighed and pulled the handle on the door. I wanted to throw up immediately. The inside of the van smelled like feet and sex.

"You know good and damn well Dyson would not want me riding in this."

"You don't know shit about Dyson so don't tell me what he wants. I'm getting you home to your husband safe and sound."

Damn, so everybody knows I'm married.

Kip hopped in the van and cranked it up with no hesitation. I wanted to slap the smirk that tugged at the corners of his lips but his mentioning of Jamison unnerved me. I could see that he was enjoying the moment.

Kip pulled out the parking spot so fast my head hit the back of the seat. I pulled the strap for my seatbelt but it was jammed. When I turned to fix it, I immediately noticed a silver Mercedes CLS parked in the far corner. It was the same car that tried to run me over in Lady's parking lot.

I didn't want to think that it was a possibility because the thought was something that I never saw coming. I even tried to shake it from my mind, but the question kept dancing around in my head, *was Dyson the one who tried to kill me?*

Chapter 11

I walked up the driveway to my house with thousands of confused thoughts in my mind. I had Kip drop me off at the gas station around the corner because I didn't want him to know where I lived. I didn't trust him and now I wasn't so sure I could trust Dyson either. Some things just weren't adding up. After seeing the Mercedes in the garage, I was convinced that Dyson was the person responsible for trying to kill me. But after thinking about it, I'd received that first text message before I even met Chauntelle so now I wasn't so sure if Dyson was involved after all.

Suddenly, my phone chirped, indicating that I had a new text message. After pulling it from my purse, it didn't take long to realize that it was from my stalker. It had been a few days since a picture of me and that latest mark were sent to me. I thought whoever the stalker could be had dropped dead, but I couldn't have been more wrong. I opened the message and shook my head at what I saw.

I saw you and him not walking in the rain but fucking just the same. Wonder how your husband will feel.

I quickly deleted the message and shoved the phone in my pocket. Whoever the fuck it was knew too much information about me. I'd just left Dyson not even thirty minutes ago. The only thing I could think of as I approached my house was that I hoped like hell they wouldn't make good on their promise and contact Jamison somehow.

I didn't have too much time to think about it because there seemed to be a more pressing matter that I would have to handle immediately. My original plan was to come home and seriously think about who this unknown enemy was, but as soon as I stood on my porch, I knew that wouldn't be happening any time soon.

"What the fuck?" I said with enlarged eyes.

Noticing my front door slightly open, I quickly grabbed the small gun that I kept in my purse and held it firmly in my right hand. With my life obviously in danger, I wasn't taking any chances. Looking on the ground, I didn't notice any broken glass which would've indicated how the intruder got inside. The door also didn't look as if the lock had been picked or kicked in, so my next initial thought was that someone had used our spare key to get in. However, after picking up the flower pot that sat a few inches away and realizing the key was still underneath, I had no idea what the fuck was going on.

At that moment, I stuck my head slightly inside the door and I called out my husband's name softly. "Jamison."

When he didn't answer, I pushed the door open and decided to walk in. I needed answers. As soon as I walked inside, I noticed a pile of clothes, shoes and accessories sitting at the bottom of the steps. Surprisingly, everything belonged to me.

"What the hell?" I mumbled under my breath.

Suddenly hearing faint voices coming from the living room, I tiptoed toward them slowly. I was about to shoot the hell out of whoever had the nerve to try and rob me after all the blood, sweat and tears I pushed out to get the nice things that I wanted.

When I turned the corner with my gun exposed like a police officer, I was shocked to see Jamison sitting there watching T.V. without a care in the world.

"Dammit, Jamison. I almost shot the shit out of you. Why is the front door open and why are my things sitting at the bottom of the steps? What the fuck is going on?" I asked angrily.

Jamison grunted my way but never looked up to acknowledge me. He looked like pure shit. Desperately needing his head shaved, his beard was also wild and beastly.

"Jamison, did you hear me?"

Again, he gave me nothing. He didn't even look up at me this time. He picked up the bottle of E&J and took another swig.

"I know you fucking hear me talking to you? What the hell is going on around here?"

"How did you get home?" he finally asked calmly.

The tone of his voice was void of emotion as if he wasn't even really there. I wanted to tell him that the truck had been stolen earlier, but I knew he would've been pissed even more since I was just now telling him.

"I had Tayla bring me home because I had a little too much to drink earlier. We had a little girl bonding time at the office."

"I didn't hear a car drive up," he said while taking another sip from his bottle.

"Oh, well, umm that's because she had to stop at the gas station around the corner, so I just decided to walk home. I didn't feel like waiting," I stammered over my excuse.

He looked at me as if he could tell that I was lying. I tried to stare anywhere but at Jamison. I needed to find a way to lighten the mood somehow. Something about the energy in the house made me feel like this night could be disastrous.

"Where are the girls?" I tried to change the subject.

"Where do you think they are at midnight? They're asleep, it's a school night, remember?"

His voice was nonchalant, but at least that was better than him giving me the silent treatment. I rolled my eyes at him and even that went unnoticed. I knew it was a school night. I didn't need his reminders.

"Oh, I mean I know that. How did the banquet go? Did Jasmine win the Shining Star award?" I questioned.

Jamison snorted his nose again in a way that reminded me of that snooty ass Chauntelle. It made me want to slap the hell out of him.

"The nerve of your ass to come home at midnight and ask me about some shit that you really could care less about.

I swear your level of selfishness amazes me. Of course Malia and me didn't give a damn, but Jasmine seemed a little hurt that her trifling ass mother pulled another one of her disappearing acts. She was the only girl there without a mother actually."

"I'm sorry, I got caught up with a new client but that doesn't mean I'm not interested in the well-being of my daughters, Jamison."

"You weren't there as usual and I'm tired of explaining to everyone that my wife is a skank that rather fuck around than take care of her family. I want you to get the fuck out!" he screamed loudly.

"Look, you're obviously drunk and not in your right frame of mind. I'm not going anywhere other than to the kitchen to get something to drink, take a shower and then go to sleep. When I wake up tomorrow, you better have all my shit back upstairs where it's supposed to be."

Whenever Jamison had anything to drink he became a totally different person. He was what most people called, 'an angry drunk', but he knew better than to touch my shit just because he was having a temper tantrum.

I walked out of the room and closed the front door before going into the kitchen to pour myself a glass of wine. Looking at the refrigerator I was in for one huge ass shock.

There were pictures of Dyson and me in the club the night I met him. All of the pictures could be explained as meeting with a client, except for the one where I was giving Dyson a lap dance. I stared at them in amazement. Where had Jamison gotten the pictures? I snatched them down and turned to go back in the living room, but Jamison stood in the doorway watching me. I hadn't heard him creep up. We stared at each other for a few seconds before I decided to plea my case.

"Jamison, look, I can explain. It's not what it looks like."

The first slap he gave me stung my cheek, shocked the hell out of me actually as the pictures flew out of my hands. The quick second slap damn near rendered me paralyzed as

Jamison dug his large fingers into my skin. He held my throat in a death grip.

"You know what your fucking problem is, Mykah? You're too damn self absorbed. I should've never fucked with you. Everybody told me you weren't shit when we were younger, but I didn't listen," he stated harshly. "I should've listened to my mother who constantly told me to make you get an abortion."

His red eyes glared at me. Jamison had left the building and I was now stuck in close quarters with a mad man.

"Ow! Jamison, you're hurting me," I managed to get out in between short gasps of air.

"I'm hurting you? Do you have any idea how much pain I'm in because of you? I could've been somebody, but I decided to stick with you because you got pregnant!" he screamed at me.

His grip tightened around my neck and I felt light headed. But my instincts to fight kicked in. My hands flew on top of his and I scratched away at the fingers that had once stood as a sign of protecting me from danger. The more my fingernails drew blood, the harder he would squeeze.

"Yeah, this is how you like to be treated. I know you're running around town dishing out your pussy for everybody, whore. I'm not stupid, Mykah. I know you're not always working late. I even called the Colliseum the other night looking for you, and you know what. They had never even heard of your ass."

"Jamison, please."

"Fuck that. I tried to respect your ass, but I guess that wasn't good enough for you."

Suddenly, I gathered enough strength to head butt him and almost passed out myself. When Jamison finally released his grip, I held my throat and coughed madly, desperately trying to control my breathing.

"Oh my God, are you fucking crazy?" I whimpered seconds later. I could taste my own blood in my mouth.

Jamison didn't respond as he grabbed my hair and dragged me across the floor toward the foyer. I attempted to fight him as he opened the front door, but none of my blows could match the adrenaline that gassed him up. He picked me up and threw me roughly on the porch. My belongings quickly followed, hitting the dirt causing a tiny cloud of dust to fly up.

"I'm done with you, Mykah. You're no longer welcome in this house."

"Jamison, you can't throw me out my own damn house," I said just before hopping up. I ran towards him.

"Watch me. I've already changed the locks and the security code. If you come here again, I won't hesitate to call the police and tell them what a trifling bitch you are."

I stopped in my tracks and looked at him questioningly.

"Yeah, that's right. I know all about the shit you're into. I've known all along, but didn't want to believe that you would stoop so damn low. But now I know your ass is capable of anything just to get some dick."

"What? What are you talking about?"

I wondered how the hell Jamison had found out about what I did for a living. I knew that he was investigating the murders for his so called book, but there was no way he could've figured out that I was the person responsible.

"I trusted you. You're the mother of my fucking kids? I can't believe you could do some shit like this. I knew your father fucked up your head a long time ago, but now you've gone too damn far. I can't even look at you. You ain't shit to me anymore."

I thought I'd done a good job with keeping my secret life private, but now it was all over. Jamison was the one person I never wanted to find out. As powerful as I thought I was, I was no match for the rage that fueled my husband. At this point, I couldn't do anything but surrender to the fact that he was done with me.

"I'm sorry, Jamison. I was just doing what I thought was best for our family."

As tears suddenly rolled down my cheeks, I didn't even bother to wipe them away or the snot that hung from my nose. I was heartbroken. I never thought that Jamison would ever get the strength to actually leave me.

"Best for your family? Are you serious? How is doing something like that best for your family? Besides, you don't give a shit about this family. You're not fooling me with them fake ass tears, you're only sorry because you got caught. Now get the fuck away from my house."

Mentioning the family seemed to make him madder. As Jamison went back into the house, he grabbed the rest of my things and started throwing everything out. The swing of his arm was like a professional baseball player.

"Jamison, please stop. I said I was sorry."

"You've been sorry, Mykah. Everybody could see it but me," he said.

Now, my tears and screams were uncontrollable because I knew it was over for sure. I was angry. I looked around for something to grab and hit him with, but there weren't any weapons within arms' reach. I had no more energy left. I needed help from someone and I needed it as soon as possible. I never tried to involve the girls in our mess, but this time I had no other choice but to yell for them.

"Malia, Jasmine help! Please, come help me!"

"You can stop wasting your time because they're not coming to help your ass. They hate you just as much as I do."

Those words pierced my heart like a sharp knife. By now I was in a full-blown sob.

"I'm…sorry. I'm so sorry," I pleaded.

"You should be sorry, Mykah. This is your fault. I tried to warn you time and time again."

At that moment, I looked at the window in the living room and saw Malia standing there watching us. I was expecting her to show some type of emotion or even give me just a little bit of pity, but she gave me none. My heart sank to my feet and I held my head down to hide my bucket of tears. Instead of consoling me, Malia laughed loudly as if she were watching a comedy show.

"I have nowhere to go, Jamison. Just let me come in tonight and I promise I'll be out first thing in the morning."

"Hell no," he shouted.

Out of the blue, Jasmine appeared behind her father. The look in her eyes told me she still loved me. She was nothing like Malia or Jamison. I truly believed I could save our relationship if given the chance.

"I love you, Jasmine," I shouted.

Malia pushed her out of the way blocking me from seeing her anymore.

I tried once again to get back in the house, but this time I was met with a kick to my stomach. I doubled over in pain.

"I still can't fucking believe that you drugged me. If you did that shit to me once ain't no way in hell I would let you back into this house so you can do it again. Jasmine is the only reason I didn't call the police on your ass!" Jamison yelled before slamming the front door.

My mind was all over the place, but at that moment I finally realized that Jamison wasn't talking about the murders. He was actually talking about the drugging incident. I was somewhat relieved that he hadn't figured out everything I was up to; even though drugging him was just as bad. I never wanted him to know what I'd done and Malia would have a lot of damn questions to answer once I got her by herself. I knew she was the one who'd told him and I would straighten her ass out sure enough.

Chapter 12

"She's asleep right now. It's been a week since she got here, but I just can't bring myself to tell her. She's been through enough shit as it is."

I stopped doing one of my sit up's in midair, wondering who Tayla was talking to about me. I grabbed my towel and wiped the sweat from my face. I then stood up and tiptoed to Tayla's door and peeked through the small crack. She looked like a nervous wreck as she paced the floor back and forth in her robe. I could hear her shower running in the bathroom. I hadn't even heard her come through the door earlier. She'd barely been around the entire week. I could only guess that she was staying over her mystery man's house or maybe some crazy ass overnight church retreat. The odd thing was Tayla didn't really have a lot of conversation for me when she was home.

"Look, I'll tell her tonight, I promise. I have to finish getting ready. I love you baby, see you soon," she said before hanging up.

Tayla sat down at her vanity and quickly took a huge gulp from her silver flask. Curious, I wanted to rush in and confront her about the conversation, but had no energy left inside of me. My life had crumbled all around me and dealing with Tayla right now would have to go on the back burner. I knew there must be something serious going on because her townhouse was damn near empty. I didn't want to think that she was possibly on drugs or something, but I couldn't think of any other reason she'd obviously sold all of her shit. When I turned to creep away, my arm hit the doorknob causing the door to push open slightly. She spun around and looked at me in shock.

"Mykah, what are you doing? I thought you were asleep."

"I was and then I woke up. That's generally what people do who aren't dead," I stated flatly.

She laughed a little but the sound seemed forced and fake as hell. When Tayla noticed I hadn't joined in, she quickly straightened her face.

"I was just about to hop in the shower."

"I figured that much. So, what, that phone call held you up?" I questioned.

"Oh no, that wasn't anyone important but I really need to catch the hot water before it goes out."

Tayla was nervous and a horrible liar. That was the main reason I never asked her to join in the business with me. She was easier to read than a remedial book.

"What's going on with you?"

"Nothing, why you say that?" she questioned defensively.

"Well, for starters you looking all around like you're paranoid, and your damn house is one area rug away from being empty. You can't even look me in my eyes."

Tayla paused and looked up in the mirror at me. I could tell she was trying to choose her words wisely before speaking.

"I'm good, Mykah. The Lord supplies me with all that I need. You don't have to worry about me. I've just been taking some of my things over to my boo's house that's all. We're planning on moving in together."

"Moving in together? Wow...before marriage? Now I may be a heathen to you, but even I know that's a sin to live with a man before exchanging vows. Aren't you worried about going to hell Ms. Church Girl?"

I smiled...she didn't.

"Please don't mock my relationship with God. I only answer to Him, not you," Tayla shot back at me.

"Yeah, okay, I'm going back to sleep. I wouldn't want to upset God's newest warrior," I said, turning to walk out of the room.

I waited on the other side of the door for a few minutes. After making sure that Tayla was definitely in the shower, I went to the vanity and grabbed her cell phone. Of course there was a password on it as I tried every combination of numbers I could think of that was associated with her in some way.

Frustrated without getting any results, I put the phone down. I was tripping anyway. It was none of my business who she was on the phone with, or maybe it was. Whatever Tayla's secret was, had somehow spilled its way in my life and it nagged the back of my mind.

I walked towards the door again, but the buzzing of her phone stopped me in my tracks. I spun back around and picked it up. My hands shook and the rage that instantly shot up inside of me almost caused my head to spin. I hit the answer button.

"Well, how nice of you to call."

The dead silence on the other end before the disconnection angered me even more. I tried to press the button to call back, but the phone locked up again. Furious by this point, I threw it against the wall and watched as it crumbled into several pieces.

Within minutes, Tayla ran from the bathroom still soaking wet with the towel wrapped around her. She looked at the broken phone on the floor and then up at me questioningly.

"Mykah, what the fuck happened? Why did you break my phone?"

"I'm sorry, it was ringing. I tried to bring it to you, but my hands must've been slippery, and it fell," I lied calmly.

I decided to treat her like I would an assignment and try to feel her out first. I knew there was no way that Tayla would come flat out and admit that she wasn't shit, so there was no other choice but to play games.

"Who was it?" she asked nervously.

I shrugged my shoulders. "I don't know. It was anonymous."

"Oh, probably a bill collector," Tayla said as she began to dry herself off.

After going back into the bathroom for a few short minutes, she came back into the room with a long t-shirt on. Tayla sat back down at her vanity and pulled out her makeup case. I could tell by how jittery she was that her nerves were completely on edge. She was definitely up to something. As she tried to put on her Mac, Ruby Woo lipstick her hands shook so badly even her cheek received some of the color. She avoided my stare down for as long as she could before finally looking up. We immediately locked eyes. Mine were begging her to tell me whatever the big secret was and hers were full of shame. She smiled a little and then focused back on her makeup.

"I don't think bill collectors call this late at night, Tayla."

"Well maybe it was someone playing on the phone," she responded. "Anyway, I'm going out tonight. I cooked some food so feel free to get a plate."

"Thanks. So, who are you going out with?"

I had my suspicions, but didn't want to believe it. Our relationship seemed so strained lately and the phone call didn't make it any better. Because of that I couldn't ignore what my gut was telling me any further. Tayla, my best friend and sister for more than half of my life had betrayed me. Again she stared up at me. I held my breath waiting on her to spill the beans. She took another gulp from her flask before speaking.

"Just a friend."

"A friend huh? Where y'all going?"

"Damn, Mykah, you acting like I'm your child or something. What's up with all the questions?" Tayla asked defensively.

I was trying to be cool about the situation, but the nerve of her to try and catch an attitude with me when she was the one in the fucking wrong, set me off.

"Let's cut the bullshit, I know exactly what you been up to!" I yelled.

I walked closer to her hoping she could feel some of the pain that I felt in my heart. Everyone in my life had seemed to let me down in one way or another, but I never would've placed Tayla into that equation.

"I don't know what the hell you talking about. I've been nothing short of a miracle in your fucking life right now. I opened my home and offered you a shoulder to cry on and now you on this paranoid shit."

Tayla looked at me as if I'd really popped a few screws, but I still wasn't convinced that she was little miss gracious host. I now knew her dirty little secret and she was going to pay for even thinking about crossing me.

"See, I didn't even really want to go here with you but I finally put the pieces of the puzzle together now. All this creeping around shit and hushed phone conversations. I bet you do have your home open for me just so you can creep over to mine and fuck my husband."

Her eyes widened. "Excuse me? Are you insane, Mykah? Look, I know you've been going through a lot lately, but you must be crazy if you think I want Jamison," she replied incredulously.

I shook my head. "No, I'm right on the money with this one. The man you been keeping under wraps is mine. That's how Jamison knew I drugged him. It wasn't Malia…you told him and you also gave him those pictures of me, you backstabbing bitch."

"I can't believe this shit. Mykah, I'm sure you have a long ass list of enemies out in the street, but I'm not one of them. You're not gonna blame me for karma giving your ass exactly what you deserve. I told your ass to quit a long time ago or this would happen."

I grabbed Tayla's thick arm and spun her around to face me. Before I knew it, my hand came down hard on her cheek. Her head flung back and she grabbed her face stunned. I could've easily continued until I beat her senseless, but Tayla wasn't a fighter. That would've been too easy.

"You've always been jealous of me, Tayla. I knew it, but I never thought you would stoop this damn low just to walk in my shoes. You better thank God that I have too much love for you to end your life, fake ass bitch!" I spewed at her.

I needed to get the fuck out of the room before I changed my mind about beating her ass or even worse…ending her life. Then again, she wasn't worth the hassle of removing the evidence. Now that I knew she was the one who'd poisoned Jamison's mind, I could just convince him that she was lying. I turned to walk out so I could pack my bags and head home.

"I'm not fucking Jamison, Mykah. I didn't even know anything about Dyson until after that night when the pictures were taken so how could I send those to Jamison you stupid bitch!" Tayla screamed at my back.

I paused for a moment and realized she was right, but why was Jamison calling her. And why was she on the phone with him earlier discussing me? I spun back around to face her for the answers.

"I heard you on the phone with Jamison talking about me, and he called you back while you were in the shower. So, you may not have sent the pictures, but everything else I'm right about."

Tayla threw her head back and laughed at me like a madwoman. I glared at her until she got the laughter out of her system.

"You know Mykah, you may have had a life that I wish I had, but I would never want to be you. You're so fucking paranoid that you just ruined our friendship, our sisterhood. You ruin everything you touch like some type of curse. I swear on my fucking life that I've never and will never look at Jamison in that way."

"You can say whatever the hell you want to, but I saw that Jamison called you with my own two eyes. So yeah, it's a little chilly on your side of the room because the shade is all over your skank ass. I'm going to get my man back."

"Okay, so it's true that Jamison called me today and a couple times this week, but that was just to check up on your ass even though you have made a complete fool out of him. And here's some grand parting words for your ass because you're leaving my shit immediately. It's your father that I'm seeing, not your husband," she said before storming to the bathroom and slamming the door.

I stood frozen, unable to move after what I'd just heard. *I can't believe this shit...Tayla and Michael together as a couple? So, is that why she's so into church now because she's fucking the pastor?*

The thought of that sick shit swirled around in my head and nosedived into the pit of my stomach. She of all people knew how evil that man was. Now I knew I should've killed his ass the night my mother died. He was the one who was cursed and would ruin Tayla's life just like he did mine.

I stumbled out of her room in disbelief. I immediately began to pack up my things that I brought with me. I grabbed my cell phone off of the table and headed down the steps so I could leave. My phone chirped letting me know that I had a text message. Before I even looked at it, I knew that it would be about some bullshit. I opened it with shaking hands and stared so hard at the words that the words bled together.

Your ending is closer than you think.

I put my hand in my purse and felt around for my gun before stepping outside. I didn't know who the fuck I could trust anymore and it was a scary feeling.

Chapter 13

"Mama where you going?" I asked in a scared tone.

I held onto her leg and she quickly shook me loose. She'd been popping Prozac pills all day long and even though I was only eight years old, I knew that her getting behind the wheel could end horribly, especially since night after night I had to help her into bed since Michael never made it home until just before the sun rose. She'd been diagnosed with severe depression and her doctor didn't do her any good. He pumped her with pills to numb her pain but to me they seemed to make her sadder.

"I'm sick of this shit, baby girl. I'm going to knock on that hoe's door and get my man. Enough is enough. They must think I'm some kind of punk bitch or something," she slurred her words as she put her winter coat on.

"Don't you ever take no shit from no man when you get older, you hear me, Mykah? If I find out you taking some shit, I'm gone kill you myself," she warned.

"Yes ma'am," I said through a cracked voice.

"And stop all that crying. If a man think you weak he gone run all over you."

She grabbed her pill bottle off the side table, popped a few in her mouth and swallowed. She'd become a pro at pill popping so water wasn't needed. When she left, I ran to the door and pressed my face against the screen.

"Mama! Please don't go! Come back, Mama, please!" I cried and pleaded.

"Mykah, wake up, baby," Dyson said, pulling me from my dream of the last time I saw my mother.

I sat up in the bed and tried to gather my thoughts. The revelation from Tayla brought up a lot of emotions I thought I'd buried somewhere deep inside of me. Feelings that I never wanted to deal with again. My mother's death had changed my life completely and solidified my hatred for Michael. It was a night I could never forget even when I tried. I used to dream about that night all the time but since the murders began, the dreams stopped.

"Mykah, are you okay?" Dyson asked.

I looked at him and smiled. I'd called him the night before and asked if he would let me crash at one of his spots until I figured something out. He was happy to assist by letting me stay at his apartment in the Tower Grove area. I still had my doubts about Dyson and his possible involvement with the silver Mercedes. But at the same time, I was glad that he seemed to be the only person I could count on lately. I felt a tug at my heart that reminded me that Jamison used to be that person. I missed my family.

"Yeah, I'm good. Just a bad dream. No big deal," I answered.

"You sure? The dream seemed real deep."

He pushed my wet hair behind my ear and pulled the blanket up around me. It was just another gentle gesture by him that made me question how he could be the monster that the streets made him out to be.

"Just some old stuff, nothing I really like thinking or talking about."

"Oh, I can dig that. We all have a past, but if you want to talk just know that I'm here for you," he replied.

"Thank you, I truly appreciate it, Dyson."

"I know you going through a rough time right now and I just want to let you know, I got you. There's something about you that I just can't get out of my system," Dyson said hoarsely.

I looked up at him good for the first time since waking up and he looked like shit. His shirt was soaking wet from sweat and it looked as if he was about to pass out any second.

"Are you okay, Dyson? You look sick," I asked with concern.

"I'm good baby. Just feeling a little bit under the weather, but I can handle it. You have enough to worry about, so don't add me to that equation."

I was going to press him further but my phone rang. I looked at the screen and saw Lady's name pop up. She wasn't big on talking on the phone, so I knew something was wrong.

"Umm I need to take this call."

"Cool, go ahead," Dyson replied.

I turned around to walk away.

"Why can't you take it right here? Is it your husband?"

Dyson had never questioned me before so I was completely thrown off guard. "No, it's not."

"Then why can't you answer it right here?"

I didn't have time to keep going back and forth, so I decided to answer. Taking a deep breath, I braced myself for whatever Lady had to say.

"Hello."

"I don't know what the fuck is going on, but I just checked my freezer and that shit looking dry. I thought you were going fishing a long fucking time ago," she hissed in the phone.

Going fishing was her code for killing a motherfucker. I couldn't talk like I wanted to with Dyson staring down my throat. I knew there was no way that Lady would be satisfied with any answer I gave her, other than I'd completed the job.

"I haven't gone fishing yet, but I think I'm going to do that soon." It was the only reply I could give her.

"It's a sad ass day for you, Mykah. What the fuck taking so long? I know good and damn well you not marinating cat for the fish to eat because that shit is backwards as fuck."

I looked at Dyson who continued to stare at me. He seemed to be really interested in my conversation. I knew that not being able to respond properly was only going to piss Lady off further. All I've ever wanted to do was please her…make her proud.

"I don't need a lesson on how to fish so please chill out. I'll call you when I'm ready," I said to her.

"Some shit's going down. It's real important that I see you."

"I'll call you later," I ended, then hung up.

"You fish?" Dyson asked me as soon as I disconnected the call.

I didn't feel like being interrogated by him now so I quickly came up with a lie to get him off my back.

"That was my father. We were supposed to go fishing this weekend. It's something he enjoys to do, so I always just suck it up and go."

Dyson seemed to be satisfied with the answer as he took the bottom of his shirt and wiped the sweat off of his face. He didn't give me a response. Instead, he laid back and closed his eyes. The sweat continued to pour off his body. It kind of scared me to see him like that.

"Dyson, are you sure you're okay?" I asked full of concern.

"I'm good, baby. Don't worry about me," he returned.

I crawled on the bed and snuggled under his arm wondering if Lady really had something important to discuss with me. I laid my head on Dyson's chest and listened to each shallow breath he took. I had my suspicions when I first met him but I was now one hundred percent sure that I could trust Dyson. I couldn't explain the connection that I felt with him but it was natural, almost as if we had connected before maybe in a previous life. There was definitely some sort of familiarity with us together.

As if he could read my thoughts, he wrapped his arms tightly around me and sighed.

"I could spend the rest of my life like this," he whispered to me.

I looked up at him and gazed into his eyes. There was no deception creeping around. I believed every single word he spoke. I placed a soft kiss on his lips but he took things further by inserting his tongue into my mouth.

"Would it be crazy and too soon for me to say that I think I'm falling for you?" he asked me once he broke the kiss.

He unbuttoned my shirt and pulled it off my arms. That little movement seemed to take a lot of energy from him. He leaned back against the pillow again and stared at me. His body was depleted but the look of desire in his eyes let me know that he wanted me. I wiped the sweat from his nose and shook my head at him.

"No, I feel the same way," I responded as I tried to unbuckle his pants.

It didn't take long for him to come out of all his clothes allowing me to notice a mark on his arm with a weird shape. I caressed it, asking, "A war mark?"

"A birthmark," he told me pulling me on top of him and sliding my thong to the side.

I unhooked my bra and allowed my breasts to fall down towards his face. He held out his tongue and licked at my hardened nipples. The sensation caused me to gyrate my hips until I could feel him stiffen underneath me. I allowed my hand to slip down toward his massive piece. I smiled in appreciation. No matter how many times we sexed each other, I was still shocked by how well packaged he was.

"Show me how much you love me then," he said.

I positioned him in my center and eased down slow and soft. He gripped my hips and helped me receive every inch of him. Unlike the first session when we got down, I caught on quickly to his size and worked my muscles up and down his shaft. He closed his eyes and allowed me to have my way with him. I took my time hitting his ass with moves that would have made a whore proud.

He could barely handle the way my ass cheeks clapped against his dick as I bounced up and down on him. The muscles in his thighs tensed and relaxed rapidly.

"You want me to love you like this?" I asked him

"You damn right, baby. Do that shit," he said back to me.

When my back arched involuntarily and trembles began to take over, I leaned down and placed my mouth on top of his. His hands grabbed my ass with as much strength as he could muster. We were both on the verge of releasing at the same time. With a common goal in mind, we both gave all that we had. I screamed loudly as I covered him with my love. I closed my eyes tightly, which was a big mistake because an image of Jamison popped in my head, killing my mood.

I slid off Dyson and tried to get my breathing together. He was a total mess, covered in sweat and sex juice. He made no moves at all to wipe his face. The way he was breathing actually started to scare me a little.

"Dyson, are you sure you ok?" I asked him again.

"Yes, baby. These long nights with no sleep are just getting to me a little. My Pops breathing down my damn back about getting shit in order because he wanna retire. I'm looking at other avenues though and that shit just starting to take a toll on me."

"I get the feeling your pops not the kind of man who would let you take your own avenues. That night he busted in on us, you almost fell on your damn face running after him."

He leaned up and pulled up his pants and looked at me as if he felt disrespected somehow.

"First of all, I ain't run after no motherfucking body, second of all, Preston LaRue may scare a lot of people but he for damn sure don't scare me. It's only because of me that shit still afloat. He just about lost his damn mind, running around after some young pussy. He ain't hardly the man no more," Dyson said angrily.

It was obvious that I had struck some sort of chord with him and the nice and gentle Dyson was now gone. I made a mental note to never mention Preston to him again. It kind of just showed me that even though we were both declaring our love for each other, we still didn't know a lot about each other.

I had all but lost my family behind him and I couldn't even tell someone what his favorite color was. I had to get a grip on this situation somehow. I did feel some strong sense of love for him but that couldn't compare to what I felt for my family.

"Damn, I didn't mean to ruffle any feathers. I don't fuck with my daddy so I guess I don't know the first thing about that kind of relationship. I'm sorry."

"It's cool baby, my Pops is just sort of a sore subject for me," Dyson replied.

"Hey, you don't owe me any explanations. We good but I need to take a shower. I hope you have some soup because I'm going to make you some when I come out and then I'm putting you in the bed and cutting that phone off so you can get some much needed rest. When is the last time you did that?"

I placed a kiss on his lips and walked towards the bathroom with my cell phone in my hand. I felt so conflicted about what to do with the Dyson situation. I wanted the money so that I could get my family back, but I also wanted Dyson on the side. It normally took me less than a week to handle my business with these men, but Dyson had already passed that mark. Chauntelle had texted me relentlessly for the past two days and I had yet to return her call. Contrary to what she believed, she was at the bottom of my list for me to give a fuck about. Right now my mind was on my family.

I needed to call my house and see if I could get someone on the line. Jamison still wasn't answering his cell phone, and Jasmine and Malia's phones always went straight to voicemail. The house phone was the last option. I closed the bathroom door and locked it before turning on the shower to drown out my conversation. After dialing my house number, I waited impatiently for someone to answer.

"Hello."

"Hey, Jasmine is that you?" I said in the phone excitedly.

"Hey, Mama. When will you be back from working?" she asked me.

Hearing her voice brought tears to my eyes. I missed her so much. It seemed like years since the last time I last saw her. Jamison had obviously told her I was working instead of telling her he wasn't allowing me to come back, or see them.

"It won't be long, baby. I promise. In fact I'm gonna try and pick you up from school tomorrow and take you shopping."

"I would really like that. Plus, there's something really important that you need to…" When she paused, I could hear a bit of a scuffling in the background.

"Jasmine, is everything okay? What is it that you need to tell me? Who is that talking in the background?"

I could hear a woman hollering in the background. I immediately recognized the drunken slur as that of Jamison's mother, Lucille.

"It's Granny. She's been here since you left and boy am I ready for her to go home. She's been drunk every day," Jasmine whispered into the phone.

Jasmine didn't know it, but hearing that she had to put up with Lucille's drunk ass made me feel even worse. If I was there it would be no way in hell that she would be in my house.

I can't believe Jamison, I thought. He knows how I feel about that shit. She's never been around my family, and she shouldn't start now.

"Listen baby, I'll be home soon and as soon as I do, she'll be the first thing to go," I assured her.

"Another empty promise coming from you, I see," Malia said into the phone.

She'd apparently wrestled it from Jasmine's grip. She really was becoming an evil seed. A part of me knew that her heart had only become hardened due to my absence so I had no one to blame but myself.

"Hey, Malia. I miss you honey."

"I bet you do. Why are you calling here?"

"I need to talk to your father, not that I have to answer to you, little girl."

She laughed loudly at me. I stared at the phone in disbelief. Her disrespect was getting way out of hand.

"My father is out on a date not that I have to answer to you either. Do all of us a favor and stop calling here."

"Listen, Malia, I swear when I get my hands on you…"

"Listen, bitch, nobody wants you in this house so stop calling here!" she yelled, cutting me off.

I stood in total shock as Malia hung up the phone. I don't know why anything she did surprised me though. She'd been disrespecting me a lot lately, clearly not the sweet little girl that I raised anymore. I tried to call back but she'd taken the phone off the hook.

I cursed under my breath, cut the water off in the shower, then quickly opened the bathroom door. I looked for Dyson in the room, but he was gone. I walked out into the living room but stopped in the hallway when I heard him talking to someone.

"Man, I got a bad feeling about this bitch. I don't trust her, you gotta think with your head and not your dick," the voice said.

I didn't have to see his face to know it was Kip hating on me as usual. Just hearing his voice pissed me off further.

"I don't tell you how to run your dick so don't tell me what to do with mine," Dyson replied.

"I'm just saying, you already know how shiesty that bitch is. She cheating on her man so she ain't loyal. Why you holding her lying ass down?" Kip asked.

"Look man, what her and her husband got going on don't have shit to do with me. You act like I've never fucked a married woman before."

"I never said that, but I am saying that you ain't never fell for one of those bitches before either. Ole girl got yo' nose wide open and she don't even compare to Chauntelle. They not even in the same league," Kip added.

Fuck your gorilla looking ass, I thought to myself.

"Now I know yo' ass tripping for real. Thanks for bringing the package, I was feeling sick as shit but you have to bounce," Dyson replied.

I was kind of hurt that he didn't defend me against Chauntelle. I may not have had the beauty she possessed, but I was no mud duck.

"Well look, I really need to know if you still want me to handle that little business for you?" Kip asked him.

"Yeah, man. If we don't hit her first, she'll hit us."

"I just want to make sure you're sure about this."

"Look, I don't need a lecture about loyalty right now. Besides, that bitch ain't loyal to me. Just do what I'm paying you for and make sure it's done. I don't have time for enemies, so end this shit right," Dyson roared at him.

I wondered who they were trying to get rid of and just what in the hell was going on with Dyson. Sweat poured down from his forehead like he'd been basking in hundred-degree weather.

"Alright, man. You don't have to question my loyalty to you. I'm gonna go handle this business. Go ahead and get back to your latest fling," Kip said.

Dyson walked him to the door and let him out. I was about to join him in the living room, but decided to hang back to see what Kip had brought him. He quickly went to the table and opened the small black package. I watched in horror as he pulled a needle out and stuck his arm with it. He sat there for a few seconds before closing his eyes.

Standing there in complete shock, I couldn't believe that Dyson was a fucking junkie. I'd ruined my marriage and family all because I had fallen for a junkie. I shook my head as I tip toed back to the room that I thought I would be staying in for awhile. Everything in my life had started to crumble just as Tayla predicted.

I'd really lost my mind for a little minute believing that I could actually have Dyson and Jamison in my life at the same time. After what I just witnessed I knew that I should have fought harder to stay away from Dyson but I now had the perfect way to kill him off, get that money from Chauntelle and still get my family back.

At that moment a text came through from Lady: Get up with me soon....Life or death situation.

Chapter 14

No sooner than Dyson dozed off, I called a cab then hauled ass out of his apartment and when they arrived minutes later, I headed to the airport. Since the police or Dyson's boys still hadn't had any luck with finding my truck, I was left without a permanent ride for me to maneuver as I pleased.

Lady had sent a text message demanding that I come see her immediately at the senior citizen building. I was certain the spontaneous visit was for a lecture about how I was bullshitting with killing Dyson. His death would be a pretty big pay and I knew she wanted her money. As much as I didn't want to hear her bullshit, I knew that if I didn't show up or showed up late, there would be hell to pay. Lady also informed me that she had some important information about Dyson and Chauntelle. I was kind of nervous because the LaRue family seemed to be full of unwanted surprises for me, so I prayed there wasn't some type of bounty on my head. I knew when I first met Chauntelle I should've sent her ass on her way. I hadn't encountered a normal day since.

When my phone rang, I looked down to see Tayla calling me once again. She was relentless and irking the fuck out of me with her persistence. The nerve of her to be in a relationship with Michael. It really bothered me. I didn't give a damn about his so called, new lease on life. I didn't believe that he turned his life around and was now such a good man. Karma didn't work like that and the bullshit that he'd put me and my mother through meant that he had a destiny with the gates of hell. Even though I had no words for her nor did I have the energy to discuss the situation about Michael any further, I snatched up the phone and answered angrily anyway.

"Why do you keep calling me?"

"Mykah, I really feel bad. We need to talk."

"There's nothing to talk about, Tayla. You been talking about this so called love of yours for the longest time, but you failed to mention it was Michael. You know what kind of person he is, what the fuck is wrong with you?"

"I know what kind of person he was and he's not like that anymore. Not since he found Christ. He wants to see you and apologize. The new Michael is caring and loving."

I looked at the phone like it was a foreign object.

"Are you crazy? He's a fucking wolf in sheep's clothing. If his ass is preaching the gospel, it's because he robbing his own damn church blind. Everything he does has a motive."

"Please, Mykah, I really love him and you know I love you, too. I just want to make it right for the both of you."

You mean, for you, Tayla. You knew how I would feel about this. You were there, Tayla for every beating he gave me, every tear I fucking cried, every lonely night that I missed my mother…you were right there so you know how fucked up he is! He cheated on my mother! He's the reason why she's dead!" I screamed into the phone.

She sat there for a moment. I thought maybe she'd hung up when she spoke again.

"You're right, I was there and I'm sorry for all the things the devil made him do to you but Michael is a different man now. We've all done some shit that ain't right, but that doesn't mean we are bad people who God can't forgive. Besides, he wants to see you so you both can finally heal."

I stared at the phone again in disbelief. This bitch had really flipped her lid and I'd reached my limit of trying not to really go in on her ass like she deserved.

"Listen, you delusional fake ass saint. Nothing about what that man did to me says that I should forgive him. Do I look like this so called God that you're always talking about? I'm never forgiving his ass and I won't forgive you for this shit either."

"You won't win this fight, Mykah. I get that Lady has gassed you up, have you running around doing the devil's work, but you should just fall back and let God handle this. His judgment comes when he feels it is necessary," she stated firmly.

"Look, I don't have time to wait for his judgment. Here on Earth, I'll play the prosecutor, judge and fucking jury. Hopefully when that time arrives, you'll finally come to your senses and stand on the right side. If not, then I guess you'll get to see your God a whole lot sooner than you plan to."

"I honestly can't believe you're judging me. You should really take a good look in the mirror, Mykah. I guess because you on a mission to kill the memory of your father in every one of the men you've killed, that makes what you've done acceptable."

"Fuck you, Tayla," I said before ending the call.

I didn't give a damn about her or Michael. I had my own family to worry about and as soon as I wrapped up this business with Chauntelle, I will put us back together again.

Surprisingly when I turned the corner onto Lady's street a few minutes later, I was hit with the glaring lights of the police and fire department. Lady's building was on fire.

"Oh my God!" I said, quickly parking the car.

I hopped out looking for Lady through the crowd of people. But the thick smoke in the air mixed with the chaos made finding her impossible. When I tried to make my way closer to the building, a short, stocky fireman immediately stopped me.

"Ma'am you can't go any further."

"But I'm trying to find my aunt. She lives in this building!" I yelled.

"Most of the people in the building have been evacuated."

I looked up, noticing the fire was completely out of control.

"What do you mean *most*? What happened?"

"A fire broke out in an apartment on the third floor. It's still a few trapped people up there, but don't worry we'll surely get them out," he replied.

My heart sunk when I heard him say the third floor since that's where Lady's apartment was. I tried to keep my cool, but my heart raced with each passing second.

"What apartment number?" I asked frantically.

"I don't know, ma'am. I'm sorry," he responded. "Please move around to the back of the building where it's safer. The individuals who were already evacuated are back there as well," he added then turned around to speak to someone else.

I walked towards the back to see if there was at least one familiar face in the crowd. It didn't take me long to bump into Lady's grandson, Rick. He was covered in smoke and blood from fresh wounds

"Oh my goodness, Rick. Where's Lady?" I asked frantically.

He limped past as if he didn't hear me. Even though his mouth was moving, I couldn't make out what he was saying. I grabbed Rick's arm and pulled him closer to me. He winced in pain and held his side.

"Where the fuck is Lady?"

"I don't think she made it," he whispered.

I stared at him like he was insane. "What?"

"I don't think she made it."

"What you mean you don't think she made it? Why didn't you bring her down with you?"

"Look, I don't want no trouble. He beat my ass and then tossed me out with a small package. I love my Grandma, but I needed the hit. I'm in so much pain."

He held the small package up and looked at it with tears in his eyes. I wanted to stomp his ass into the ground. He was a worthless piece of shit.

"Who beat your ass and what happened to Lady?"

I shook Rick's arm hoping that it would also shake some sense into him. I needed him to give me answers, but he was in a deep craving for a hit. Between that and the ass kicking he'd obviously received Rick seemed seconds away from dying.

"I tried to pay them back. I swear I did. The interest was just too high. She wanted to save me. Lady said she would handle it," he rambled to himself.

"Who was it? Think real hard! Lady is probably dead, fool!" I yelled at him.

Rick stared at me with no answers. He didn't have to give me one anyway because my mind drifted back to when I heard Dyson giving that order to Kip tonight. I didn't even think it was a possibility that Lady was the target at the time. My heart panicked further and I knew I was probably too late to save her. I stared at the teary eyed man and waited for him to tell me something different.

"I don't want no trouble. He said if I told anyone, I would be next."

Rick shrugged his shoulders as if there was no way he would die. Like it was okay for his grandmother to die but not him.

I smacked his hand causing the drugs that he held to fall on the ground. Rick fell down on top of them, singing to himself. He hadn't even realized that Lady's death was on his hands.

"Mykah, oh my God, Lady's place is on fire. She didn't make it out. They just brought out a body bag. People are saying it's her…They're saying it's her! Ole bless her soul, Lord!" a woman yelled at me.

I turned around and saw that it was one of Lady's neighbor's, Ms. Dorothy. She was also good friends with my mother before she died. She had tears running down her face and her hair was all over her head.

"Calm down, Ms. Dorothy."

It was a struggle for me to keep my composure, but I needed to keep my head clear. This was just too damn much for me. Lady was like a second mother and had really helped me and Michael out after the tragedy. She spent plenty of nights cooking, cleaning and helping us cope with the unbearable grief.

"She sure did love you, Mykah, just like she birthed you herself. She loved y'all like you were her own blood. I just can't believe that she's gone. Ole Lord, this can't be happening. What will we do," Ms. Dorothy continued to cry.

I felt sorry for her. If Lady truly was dead, a lot of people would be hurt. I rubbed her arm briefly trying to console her.

"We don't know for sure if it's Lady, Ms. Dorothy. I'm going to see if I can find out what happened," I told her.

"Well, what the fuck are you waiting for?"

I didn't have to turn around to know that the voice belonged to Jamison's mother, Lucille, but I turned around anyway.

"What are you doing here?" I asked. It was evident that she'd been on another drinking binge…again.

"I was coming here to play bingo with my girl if you must know my business." Lucille looked up at the building with tears in her eyes. "I can't believe this shit."

I continued to stare at Lucille as the smell of Vodka reeked through her pores. "Why the fuck are you sitting here looking at me all stupid for? Get your ass in there and see if my girl is okay, dammit," Lucille said to me.

I didn't want to make a scene at a time like this so instead of getting into a petty argument, I ran towards the front of the building. I had to find a way to see if Lady really was in the body bag that they carried out. Making my way towards one of the crowds that had formed, I instantly stopped in my tracks when I noticed the silver Mercedes parked on the side of her building. When the window rolled down, Kip looked at me with a smile on his face. He sparked his cigar, laughed and then quickly sped out of the parking lot.

I didn't even think twice about grabbing my gun and chasing after him. I cut through the side street that took me to the front of the apartments where Kip would have to drive out of. Thank God I kept my silencer on it because I'd forgotten all about the police on the other side of the building when I pulled the trigger twice, hitting his left tire.

Within seconds, his car spun out of control and hit the side of a tree. The driver's side of the car was pressed firmly against it. My adrenaline pumped wildly. I could see Kip struggling as he attempted to get out the passenger's door, but that too was smashed in. I tapped on the broken window and looked down on him with rage burning through my eyes.

"You sorry piece of shit. I should've killed your ass a long time ago," I said to him.

He looked at me and attempted to laugh. His hand rested on a piece of metal that was stuck in his stomach. Blood seeped from the corner of his mouth. I could tell from the injury that it would take one hell of a miracle to save him.

"You don't have the balls to kill me," he said.

"Don't kid yourself, asshole. I could eat a fat pussy like you for breakfast and still be starved."

He laughed again and spit a large amount of blood out of the window at me. I jumped to the side and dodged the liquid. He smirked at me and despite the brave face he tried to put on, I knew that he felt death near him. I was going to give his ass just what he needed. But first, I wanted answers because none of what was going on made much sense.

"Why did you kill, Lady? Did Dyson put you up to this?" I asked.

"I don't know what the fuck you're talking about," he returned.

"Why have you been following me? What the fuck is your purpose?"

"I ain't telling you shit. You about to find out the hard way."

"I'm not afraid of whatever comes my way. I'll always be the last bitch standing," I said to him arrogantly.

"Last bitch standing, huh? That's what you think. You done fucked over the wrong person and now you playing in the majors. That minor shit you been on, it can't even compare," he said while wincing in pain.

He was struggling just to talk but he seemed adamant on going there. Hate could fuel a person like that but what I didn't understand was why he hated me so much. I didn't even know who his ass was until I met Dyson.

"I know all about yo' ass and them murders you be laying down. I followed you and watched your ass for months. You so caught up in thinking you the damn best, you didn't have a clue."

Kip threw me for a loop with that one. I had no clue how he knew anything about what I did. I was always careful in covering my tracks. I thought back to the first night I saw his car when it tried to run me over in the parking lot. I thought it had been an accident at first. It made me wonder how I'd never seen the car before then. I took a few seconds to make sure no one was watching us. With all the commotion going on, we weren't even thought about. At that moment I knew what had to be done. I cocked my gun, but to my surprise Kip wasn't even fazed.

"Yo' dumb ass can't see the pieces of the puzzle and they're sitting right in your face. You being set up by the ultimate bitch."

"I'm not scared of Chauntelle," I roared. "And as soon as I get done killing your pathetic ass, I plan to take them all down. Starting with Dyson's weak for pussy ass."

Kip laughed again as he pulled a Newport from the pack that sat beside him on the seat. Slowly he fumbled around in his pocket until he found his lighter. He paused from the pain before lighting the cigarette up. After taking a short puff he looked at me.

"I guess you think you know Dyson since he bends you over occasionally. Dyson ain't got no real love for you. You'll be dead by the time you lay your head down tonight," he said.

"Too bad you won't be here to see it though," I returned.

He took another puff of the cigarette and coughed. Tiny trickles of blood flowed from the corner of his mouth. He wiped it away and looked at me with tears in his eyes. He knew the end was coming for him. I felt like the Angel of

Death, sitting and watching for my time to swoop in and take his miserable life.

"I don't have to see it because I already know how this shit will play out. We been planning this shit for months. You have no idea the kind of hell you about to go through. You won't have shit when this is over…"

Kip stopped talking abruptly when he was hit with another coughing fit. This time blood poured from his mouth like a fountain. His eyes rolled around and his body shook as if he was going into a seizure. I didn't want to give him the satisfaction of dying on his own, he didn't deserve a peaceful death. Not after the horrible way that he killed Lady and the way mind games he tried to play with me. I raised my gun and quickly put two bullets in his head. I watched in pleasure as his brains splattered against the dashboard and the seat.

"That was for Lady, motherfucka!" I screamed at his corpse.

As much as I was sick of death, killing Kip somehow soothed the pain that I felt. Once I got rid of Chauntelle and Dyson I knew I would feel even better but something inside of me was telling me that Kip knew a secret that I needed to figure out. I didn't have time now but I would definitely find out what he was hiding.

Seconds later, I turned and ran away just as I heard the sound of emergency personnel flood the area. I needed to get back to the parking lot to get my rental car, but decided to say 'fuck it' and left it where it was. With that many police moving around, I didn't want to be anywhere near the vicinity. I had bigger fish to fry and now that Kip was out of the way there was nothing that could stop me from killing Dyson next. It was no longer about the money and strictly for my loyalty to Lady.

Chapter 15

I sat on the side of the bed and held my banging head. It had been one hell of a night. I looked around at the empty alcohol bottles that were sprawled across the floor and tried to piece together what happened after I killed Kip. I didn't have many options of where I could go for comfort, so I called a cab and had them bring me to my house. With the clock on the nightstand reading two o'clock, I couldn't believe I'd slept that long. It was the first time I was able to sleep in my own California king size bed in a week. It felt like heaven to be back. I could've easily stayed in a plush hotel downtown, but with the way I felt about Lady's death, I needed some sort of familiarity. Lucille had more than likely informed Jamison about what happened already and that worked in my favor. He knew how close I was to her, so he had to know how much pain I was in.

I was prepared to use Lady's death to get Jamison to talk to me. I even planned to do some major begging until he told me that I could move back in. However, to my surprise, no one was home when I arrived. I knocked on the door for several minutes hoping that maybe one of the twins were there. The cab had already left and there was no way I would be able to get back into the city from Lake St. Louis so late. After several attempts to get inside, I broke the basement window, climbed inside, then deactivated the alarm. It took me a few tries to guess Jamison's new code but after putting in Lucille's birthday, the siren finally went off. I didn't understand his allegiance to her drunk ass, but was glad at the moment since it got me in the house.

Instantly, I began yelling Jasmine's name throughout the house, hoping like crazy she was asleep; wishful thinking. I simply wanted to see her face again. When I opened the door to the girl's room, a sense of guilt spread through my body. I became even more emotional and shocked when I made my way to my room and saw that a lot of my expensive clothes had been cut to shreds. The mirror on my vanity was cracked and in red lipstick there was a message for me that simply stated, *Wack Bitch*. I knew Jamison didn't write it. The handwriting belonged to Malia. Her hatred for me seemed to be growing by the second. I just stared at in shock. After the night I had, there was no energy left inside of me to do anything other than drink

We always kept the bar fully stocked so I took complete advantage of that and attempted to drink my sorrows away over losing Lady. One Patron shot quickly turned into me drinking excessively because I was devastated that I couldn't do anything to help her.

Soon my phone vibrated on the nightstand causing me to put the bottle down. I looked over at it and saw that it was Dyson. I hit the reject button and shook my head in disbelief that he had the nerve to call. If he thought I was that dickmatized that I wouldn't figure out what the fuck he'd done, he was wrong. I owed everything that I had to Lady for not only raising me but taking me under her wing. I'd failed her by falling for Dyson and then allowing him to have her killed right under my nose. He'd called me several times last night, but I didn't have the strength to deal with him and his betrayal so I ignored each call. He would definitely have to pay for what he'd done though.

"Mykah, what you doing here?"

When I turned around to my surprise I saw Tayla standing in the doorway with a backpack in her hand. She looked shocked and somewhat nervous to see me.

"I live here. What the hell are you doing here?" I asked her suspiciously. "And how did you get in here?"

Tayla sighed. I continued to stare her down waiting on the answer. First Jamison called her phone and now she was showing up at my house. It seemed to me as if I was right about the two of them messing around. She'd probably lied about being with Michael just to throw me off the truth.

"Jamison called me a few minutes ago and asked if I could pick up the girls' uniforms. They forgot them."

"Oh really? Well, they didn't come home last night. Where are they?"

"I don't know where they were. I'm sorry," Tayla responded.

I didn't believe her. I knew her sneaky ass had more information.

"How did you get in here?" I asked again.

"Jamison said the spare one was under the rug on the front porch." She looked at me and shook her head. "Damn, I already explained to you that I'm not fucking Jamison, Mykah. I don't know what else you want me to do. The girls are my Goddaughters and they've been through enough as it is, I'm just trying to help keep some normalcy in their lives."

I stared her up and down looking for a reason to believe anything she said, but I just didn't see her as my best friend anymore. She lied to me and slept with the enemy and I could never forgive her for that.

"I want you to stop fucking Michael. How about that, Tayla? That's some sick shit if you ask me. He watched you grow up and now he's your so called man. Do you know how fucking ridiculous that sounds? He watched you grow up and now y'all sleeping together!" I yelled.

Tayla put the book bag down and walked towards me. As she held her arms open for a hug, I looked at her like she was insane. Just a day earlier we'd had it out and now she wanted to hug. She was crazy as hell.

"Mykah, I'm not the enemy here. Yeah, I made a mistake but we all make them. I'm truly sorry but you carrying around this negative energy and the spirit is telling me that you need a hug," she said.

"You're right, you are sorry as hell, but that's your burden, not mine. Don't put your hands on me."

I walked past her and grabbed the bottle of Patron that had a little left in it. I turned it over and allowed the liquid to wash over me. It was the only way I would be able to get rid of the headache that pounded like a marching band.

Why are you so mad at me? I fell in love, Mykah. I know you're not so jaded that you can't see that Michael has changed and our love is real. If you believe that Dyson is such a good person, how is my situation different? Shit, he's a married man. You surround yourself with bad people all the time. You worshiped the ground Lady walked on like she was a saint, but she was nothing more than a street hustler."

"Don't fucking worry about who I'm sleeping with and if you ever speak bad about Lady again, I will kill your ass. That's a promise."

Just hearing Tayla mention Lady's name brought back the horrific memories from the night before. I wanted to forget that my current lover had taken her from my life. Before I could think anything further, tears spilled from my eyes and soaked my face. I flew into a fit of rage, fighting the air better than Tre had in *Boyz n the Hood*. Exhausted, I hit the floor and continued to cry.

"Mykah, what's wrong?" Tayla asked.

I was so caught up in my ball of hormonal confusion that I hadn't realized Tayla was now on the floor holding me. She cried along with me as I told her what happened to Lady. I kept the part about Dyson out of the equation for now. I would deal with him in my own way and time and didn't want to share anything further.

"Everything is just so fucked up right now, it wasn't supposed to happen like this," I said through tears.

"I can't believe this. I found out about the fire last night on the news, but I had no idea that Lady was the one who was killed." She rubbed my back. "I know I may not be the best person to give you advice right now, but you need to pray, girl. The devil riding you hard right now and you can't let him win. Fight back like the no-nonsense Mykah you're known to be."

"Last time I prayed for help, my mother walked out of the door and never came back. Prayer is for the naïve but you're right about one thing, I need to fight back. And I'm gonna start with getting my family back."

"I'll let your ignorance slide since you're in mourning, but you're wrong about the power of prayer. Just open your heart and listen to that tiny voice that speaks to it."

I hopped up from the floor and wiped my face with the back of my hand. It was almost as if Lady whispered in my ear for me to get my sorry ass up and handle my business. Her words of wisdom were the only spirits I needed. I had the perfect plan to get my family back. I needed to get the girls from school that way Jamison would be forced to talk to me. I knew Tayla would not be down with me doing a mini kidnap session, so I had to find a way to throw her off.

"Tayla, I feel dehydrated or something. Can you get me a glass of water please?"

"Sure. You need anything else?" she asked me concerned.

"No, that's it."

I pretended to be two steps away from passing out just so she could go move faster. As soon as I heard her hit the bottom step, I reached for Tayla's purse and grabbed her car keys. I snatched another bottle of alcohol from the bar and didn't bother sneaking down the steps as I took off running at top speed. By the time Tayla realized what was happening I was already in her car and had it started. She ran after me as I sped out the driveway on my way to the girls' school.

* * *

I circled the parking lot of Rosati Kain Catholic School waiting for the girls to come out of the building. Most of the kids had already gone for the day, but the twins always stayed late for dance practice. I'd been wrecking my brain trying to figure out where they could've stayed the night before. I called Malia and Jasmine, but neither of them would answer my calls.

I didn't have to wait long when the girls and one of their friends emerged. They looked so much older than the last time I laid eyes on them. I pushed back the tears that tugged at my eyes. I didn't want to seem unstable in front of their friend as I hopped out of the car and strutted towards them. As I got closer, my blood boiled when I noticed that their friend wasn't a kid at all but more so an evil, manipulative bitch.

"What the fuck are you doing here with my kids, Chauntelle?" I asked her angrily.

"Well, well, well if it isn't the long lost deadbeat mother," she replied to me smugly.

I gave her an evil glare. "You've really gone too far this time, bitch."

"Ma, please stop, you're embarrassing us," Jasmine stated quietly. She looked around nervously at the few people who walked past us. She didn't do well in confrontational environments.

"It's too late for that, Jasmine. Your mother has been an embarrassment. What kind of woman would miss her kids grow up while she's out there sleeping around with married men?" Chauntelle asked.

"The kind that's about to end your fucking life!" I spewed back at her.

"Oh my God, you're such a damn weirdo. Mrs. LaRue is one of the Biology teachers here, which you would know if you were the least bit interested in our academics. Why would you speak to her like that?" Malia questioned.

"Malia, mind your damn business, you're already on my list." I gave Chauntelle another look of death. I'm trying to figure out what kind of games you're playing."

"She not playing any," Malia butted in again. "You're such a bitch!"

I was beyond the point of being angry and I was mad as hell at myself for not bringing my gun with me. Chauntelle had been a great wave of bad luck ever since she first walked into my life, and Malia had just crossed a line that no one could save her from.

"I'm not playing games, Mykah. I told you from day one that I had a new life I needed to get to. It's not my fault that you didn't know it was your life that I was referring to."

"What the hell are you talking about?" I asked her. "Look, I know what this is about and I know that I'm taking longer than you expected, but I'm gonna take care of it."

Chauntelle smiled. "It's more complicated than that. Jamison and I are actually in love and I promise to be better to him than you ever were," she replied snobbishly.

I was so mad my temples began to throb. "Over your dead body will I ever allow that to fucking happen."

"What the hell are you doing here Mykah?" Jamison asked.

I jumped, startled by his voice. He looked pissed that I was making a scene outside of the girls' school.

"I came to get the girls so we can go shopping."

"They don't want to go with you, but you already know that so what's really going on?" Jamison badgered.

"No, the question that really needs to be asked is what the hell is going on with you and Chauntelle," I responded.

"What's going on with me is none of your business anymore. You made your choice and I made mine," Jamison said while nodding his head to the car.

Right on cue the girls quickly ran towards it and got in. They rolled down their windows so they wouldn't miss a word of the argument. Once I looked at the pain on Jasmine's face, I wanted to murder Chauntelle and Jamison's ass. I had other plans for Malia.

"Go away Mykah. You weren't coming to their school before so don't start now," Jamison added.

I stared at my husband. He looked so distant. While I honestly still loved him, it looked as if he hated me. "So, you choosing her over me, is that what you're saying, Jamison?"

I grabbed his arm and forced him to look at me. He was too busy eyeing Chauntelle to give me any attention.

"You forced this, not me. She was there for your kids when you wouldn't even bother to show up," he informed.

"You don't even know her Jamison. She sought you out on purpose. This is all a game for her to get back at me."

"Get back at you for what? She doesn't even know you. She's never met you because you've never bothered to show up to this school before. So how dare you come up here now and cause a huge scene in front of your kids' teachers and friends? What kind of woman are you?" Jamison asked.

I wanted to blurt it out to Jamison that Chauntelle hired me to murder her husband, but I couldn't implicate her without bringing myself down. She looked at me and smiled condescendingly before turning to Jamison.

"Baby, I'm ready to go. She's obviously delusional, I've never seen her a day in my life. I don't have time for this bullshit."

She placed her arm around his waist as he laid a seductive kiss on her lips. Chauntelle looked at me again with a smirk on her face. They looked like a couple in love. I backed away from them in complete disbelief. I hopped in the car with the intentions to pull off but watching Chauntelle with my family set something off in me. Protectively, Jamison wrapped his arm around the small of her back and held her in a firm hug. Watching them carry on was slowly killing me.

The alcohol sat warmed by the sun on the seat as I cracked the bottle open and took a long gulp. Jamison was in full-fledged gentleman mode as he made sure Chauntelle was in the car safely before he walked around to the driver's side and got in. The smile on his face was one that he used to give me when we first got together.

That green-eyed bitch had completely moved me out of the way. It was like I had no control as I fired up the engine and placed my foot all the way down on the gas.

Jamison looked over at me in horror as he realized it was too late for him to move out of the way. The screeching sound of my tires seemed to fuel me as I slammed into the side of his car pinning him behind the wheel. I don't know why I did it but I put the car in reverse and then floored the gas pedal until I hit the car again and again. The screams coming from the teachers and students on the lot were the only thing that pulled me out of my trance. With a now clear mind I looked at the mangled car and was shocked to see that my family wasn't moving. People screamed from every corner as they ran in their direction.

Still no movement inside the car.

Jamison's head hung on the steering wheel causing it to blare loudly. The girls were huddled together with glass and blood covering them. Malia was on top of Jasmine appearing to be lifeless, trying to protect her as usual. My instincts told me to get out to see if they were okay. But a woman was on her cellphone screaming to a 911 operator and pointing at me as if they could see me.

Out of the blue, the Principal appeared and opened the car door. His next set of words tore me to pieces.

"I think they're all dead. Call 911!" he shouted.

"Help! Get someone here now!"

My heart shot into hysteria and I tried to remain calm as I flew out of the parking lot. My hands shook nervously on the steering wheel.

What the fuck did I just do?

Chapter 16

"Shit! I can't believe I fucking did that," I mumbled to myself as I took another shot of Patron.

I tried to steady my hands from the twitch that had taken over, but my nerves knew I wasn't in a keep calm type of situation. An image of Jamison slumped over on the steering wheel with blood pouring from his mouth and the way the girls laid lifelessly popped in my head.

Tears flowed and the revelation that I'd killed my family out of jealousy tormented me. No matter how much I tried to think of something else, the scene replayed itself consistently.

I picked up the next shot and threw it back before the burn of the first shot had time to subside. I grabbed my cellphone and dialed Jasmine's number hoping she'd survived. The phone rang several times before rolling over to voicemail. I called Malia and went through the same thing. I shook my head as I hung the phone up. I didn't know what was going on and that seemed to be killing me softly. I guess it was poetic justice in a way.

I'd done a lot of foolish things in my life, but hitting Jamison with Tayla's car was now at the top of the list. As careful as I'd been throughout the years with disposing of men, I didn't understand how I was able to let my emotions get the best of me. It was all Chauntelle's fault. I knew not to trust that bitch as soon as she walked in. Now, Jamison was dead and I was headed to jail.

"So fucking dumb. I'm so glad Lady isn't here to see this shit," I mumbled again.

I looked around the dimly lit hole in the wall bar that was my current place of refuge. The door opened and my eyes quickly searched for who would walk in. I sat up prepared to fight my way out with the police if I had to, but two men stumbled through covered in dirt. Their hardhats were still on their heads as if they ran out of work so fast they'd completely forgotten to take them off. They made their way towards the pool table while shouting to the bartender to send them a pitcher of beer.

The place was empty for the most part with only a few people sitting at the bar watching Wheel of Fortune while they drunk away whatever sorrows they had in life. An old tune from *Bobby Blue Bland* played low on the almost broken down jukebox, and a lone roach crawled slowly up the wall inches away from my head. It looked like he didn't have a care in the world. I shook my head as I realized that I'd sunk so low that for a second I wanted to trade places with a damn cockroach.

I sat back in a booth with my eyes intently watching every move that was made. I had no one to trust. Normally, I would call Lady in a time like this, but her untimely death put a damper on that option. I needed to calm my nerves and try to figure out what my next move would be. That was kind of hard to do considering the fact that I was once again without a car. As soon as I hit the city limits from the twin's school, I ditched Tayla's car and walked a few blocks over and stopped at the first low-key spot I could find. I was certain that the police would be looking for not only me, but that vehicle as well.

My phone buzzed in my pocket scaring the hell out of me. My nerves were still shot to hell and no matter how much I wanted them to chill the fuck out. I just couldn't get it together. I took a deep breath, downed my last shot of tequila, and then looked at the illuminated screen. I hoped like hell there was some divine intervention and Jasmine was calling me back. I'd been calling her back to back since the accident. Instead, it was Tayla calling for the tenth time. I was sure that she'd gotten wind of what happened but there was no way in hell I could sit through another one of her hypocritical ass fake sermons about doing the right thing. Even if I did commit a crime in her car I still wasn't in the mood to hear her mouth. What the fuck did she know about the right thing anyway? I turned the phone off and shoved it back into my pocket.

"Would you like another shot?" the waitress asked me.

I jumped knocking over the glasses on the table. I didn't see her walk up to me because my eyes were so busy studying the front door expecting the police to bust in at any minute. Feeling stupid for being so nervous, I rolled my eyes at her before I began to speak.

"Don't fucking walk up on me like that," I growled.

"Damn, excuse me. I was just trying to see if you were good. That's my job ain't it?"

She rolled her neck at me so hard, I thought her Ronald McDonald inspired wig would fall on the floor. Her light brown arms were completely covered in tattoos and the half tarnished herringbone around her neck was just a day from giving her gangrene. I looked her up and down and came to the conclusion that she was from the south side. The south side chicks were rough around the edges and didn't mind jumping off with the quickness. I didn't want to fuck with her in the current state I was in.

"Just bring me the entire bottle of Patron, please," I said while dismissing her with a wave of my hand.

"We don't have Patron, princess. We been giving yo' ass the cheap watered down shit. You want that or what?"

I shook my head at her incredulously. At least she was honest.

"Yeah, I guess that'll do."

She sucked her teeth and gave me a small nod with her nose turned up. She had major attitude as she stumped away. I was just about to study the cockroach again but quickly sat back in shock as Lucille walked through the door.

Her face was turned up and her eyes were bloodshot red. I cowered down in the booth hoping that she wouldn't notice me sitting in the corner. I could tell from her facial expressions that her heart was heavy. I was sure it was because not only was Lady dead, but I'd also killed her son. She always told him that I would be his downfall.

"You gotta fucking be kidding me," I mumbled.

The universe was really on a 'beat Mykah's ass' kick. Of all the bars in the city, only my unlucky ass would wind up in one with the one person I didn't want to see anytime soon.

Thankfully I was given a few minutes to regroup and get my thoughts together because she sauntered right pass my booth with her eyes focused on the bar.

"Hey, Lucy Lou, what's up with cha gal?" the bartender yelled at her.

He was also the owner of the bar and guessing by the way he greeted Lucille, I could tell that she was a regular at this shitty establishment. He licked his ashy lips and stared at her as if she didn't look like drunken leftovers. I could see that I wasn't the only one who was using Lady's death as an excuse to drink. In just twenty-four hours it looked like Lucille had aged even more than her normal wrinkled face. Her short, brownie colored hair was matted and tangled and she had on the same clothes that I saw her in the night before. It just goes to show that some men don't care what's outside the V of a woman's body. As long as she could twerk it, they'll serve it. Lucille was definitely oiled up because she had a mean two step in her stagger. She swayed to the beat of the blues song on her heels.

"Ain't shit to it, Ernie, you know how I roll baby," Lucille purred at him as she spun around to show him what she was working with.

Had I not been trying to be low key, I probably would have laughed my ass off. She looked ridiculous. I covered my face with my hand and prayed that she wouldn't notice me, but I knew the gig was up when her usual disgusted frown returned to her face and she growled my way. I cursed under my breath as she made her way to the sunken red booth I sat in.

"Well, well, well look what I spy with my little eye, a skank cunt hoe bitch. Say, Ernie, baby, you letting trash in this place now?" Lucille yelled to the top of her lungs.

The waitress laughed a little too hard as she all but dropped the bottle of tequila on the table and then quickly stood back to watch the show.

"I ain't for no bullshit tonight, Lucy. Police already busting my ass for that shit you caused last time you was in here cutting up," Ernie replied back to her.

Hearing the word police caused sweat to pour down my back. The last thing I needed to do was kick her ass and have them show up and lock me up. Lucille was an unpredictable person who couldn't control her hatred for me.

"Ain't gone be no damn fighting, ain't that right, huzzy?" she asked me spitefully.

I didn't answer as she sat down in the booth, popped open my bottle and took it to the head. I watched as Lucille swished the drink around in her mouth and then spit it back in the bottle. Her eyes dared me to say something or make a move. As bad as I wanted to, I knew she had the police on her side. If I wanted to walk out without hurting her or going to jail, I was gonna have to be nice to her.

"Look, Lucille, I'm really sorry. I never…" I began to say but she immediately cut me off.

"Don't fucking talk to me like we friends. I don't fuck with you like that. I've never fucked with you. If it wasn't for Lady I would've been dusted these streets with yo' worthless ass a long time ago."

Lucille grabbed the bottle from the table again and took a long gulp. Her eyes closed as relief washed over her body. The monkey on her back needed to be fed and she continued to sip until the feeling vanished. She sat the bottle down, burped and wiped the few dribbles of tequila from her mouth with the back of her hand. She stared at me intently and I moved around nervously under her beady-eyed stare.

"You sure don't look like much. And you damn sure ain't as pretty as Beyonce. I never understood what it was about you that my boy saw cause I for damn sure don't see it. Hell maybe it's that big butt you got."

"I'm not about to sit here and let you talk shit to me. If you plan on calling the police then do it," I said while gathering my things to make a fast exit.

"I wish you stealing my boy's heart was a crime because I would've been had your ass locked up."

I stopped moving and looked at Lucille like she was crazy. I stared back at her waiting for some type of backlash for killing Jamison, but she didn't say a word about it.

Maybe she doesn't know yet, I thought. I leaned back in the booth with my newfound braveness and glared at her.

"Jamison is a grown man, not a boy. Are you still mad because he decided to be with his family. Just face it…I won and you lost. What part of that shit don't you understand?"

"Oh, I understand the shit perfectly clear. You just like yo' damn mammy, stealing men that don't belong to you because you think the world revolve around yo' ass," she replied angrily.

"You don't know shit about my mother, so shut the fuck up!" I screamed.

The few people who were in the bar turned around, placing their full attention on us. Tonight we were their entertainment which I was certain was a hell of a lot better than their own boring ass lives.

"Oh, you get mad about that shit, huh? Yo' mama thought she was the shit just like you do. Parading her ass up and down the street trying so damn hard to get caught by anybody with a hook. When that didn't work, she got real fucking desperate. She fucked and sucked her way right into Lady's man's life. Trapped that man with the oldest trick in the book, having a fucking baby."

"What? Get your drunk, babbling ass away from my damn table. Nobody wants to hear that make believe shit."

"You can take what I'm saying with a grain of salt, but here's some juicy beef you can season so you'll digest the shit better. Yo' mamma stole yo' daddy from my girl, Lady. They both wound up pregnant at the same time. Mighty funny they both went in labor at yo Daddy house on the same damn day. He and yo Grandma delivered both of them babies but Lady come out of there saying hers died and yo mama's lived. She ain't remember much 'cause something bad happened in that house and I been had my feeling that yo Mama was the cause of it. I always did think you looked more like Lady than yo Mama."

I felt tears leak from my eyes. What the fuck was Lucille's drunk ass talking about? What she was saying couldn't be possible. I was so fucked up…both mentally and heavily intoxicated.

"Are you implying that Lady is my real Mama? You crazy bitch, do you really think Michael would have stood by and watched that?" I asked her angrily.

"Michael barely knew his balls from yo mama's titties when he first got up with her. It ain't till that baby shit happened that he stopped giving a damn about her. I don't know what kind of fucking hocus pocus she had going on, but you do because you used that same shit on my boy," Lucille said then laughed cruelly.

The revelation almost knocked me out of the booth completely. But I refused to give her the satisfaction of thinking she had something on me. Even as my insides quivered, I smiled at her and put on the bravest poker face I could muster up.

"It was nice seeing your drunk ass. I'll tell Jamison to make sure he ups your life insurance policy because from the looks of it, you'll probably be dead soon."

"You bitch. I can't wait until my boy finally comes to his senses and get the fuck away from you. Yo' daddy wasn't man enough to leave yo' crazy ass mama and she ruined him. I won't let you do that shit to my boy. No way. Not over my dead fucking body."

This time I laughed at her like she was the dumb one. It had been seventeen years and she still held on to this insane hatred for me because of what Jamison could have been. As bad as I felt for hitting him, I wasn't going to take Lucille's shit. She had been nothing but a bitch to me and had she not constantly poisoned Jamison's head about me, he probably would've never turned to the arms of Chauntelle.

"I feel sorry for you, Lucille, I really do. And that day when your dead fucking body, as you called it, comes, I'll be at your funeral singing, zippity do da, to the top of my fucking lungs. Have a good day," I said, standing up to leave.

I couldn't lie…my mind was on Michael and this Lady shit. I didn't know if what Lucille said had any validity to it, but I was gonna find out. Lady being my real mother couldn't be possible. He owed me the truth for once if nothing fucking else. I knew that going to see him tonight wouldn't be a good idea though because Tayla would try to convince me to turn myself in, not to mention how pissed she was that I used her car to kill my husband.

"I'm not fucking done with you, bitch." Lucille stood up as well.

"Aye, Lucy, I told you I can't have no shit popping off in here. You gone make me lose my damn liquor license!" Ernie screamed across the room.

We both looked at him just as breaking news popped up on the television screen. As the newscaster stood in front of the twin's school, I immediately felt my heart sink to my stomach. There was broken glass scattered on the ground and the dented pole that Jamison's car hit could also be seen. Tears threatened to assault my eyes watching the damage I had done. The words DEATH AT A LOCAL SCHOOL flashed across the screen. Seconds later, a photo of Jamison flashed on the screen also, causing Lucille to scream and holler.

"Turn it up! Turn that damn T.V. up! That's my baby!"

As Ernie reached to turn the volume up, I said a silent prayer as the newscaster spoke about the possible suspect. I wasn't shocked when the next picture that popped up on the screen was mine. Lucille turned around and looked at me with hell in her eyes.

"You fucking bitch, what did…"

Those were the only words I let Lucille get out as I punched her in the face as hard as I could. Her paper-thin body fell to the ground swiftly just before I bolted for the door and ran for dear life.

Chapter 17

The sun peeked through the half closed blinds, waking me from sleep. I groaned and turned over with the flat pillow on top of my head. Despite the fact that the Grand Motel had cheap, hard sheets, I'd done nothing but sleep for the past two days.

Killing Jamison had taken all of the energy out of my body. Doing simple things like eating and bathing just seemed so exhausting. More than anything, I desperately wanted to reach out to the hospital to see if the girls were alive, or at least in stable condition. The reports stated that people died but there were no names released. Hopefully it was Chauntelle's ass.

Unable to go back to sleep, I sat up in the bed trying to decide if I wanted to turn the T.V. on. It had been off since I arrived a few days ago because I was too afraid to watch the news. I didn't want to see how horrible of a person I really was. I looked over at the cell phone on the nightstand. I wondered how many people had tried to contact me. It was still turned off because I didn't want to take the chance of the police tracking down my location. That was the problem with all this technology shit, it was easy to track everyone's move.

I grabbed my wallet and looked inside to see how much money I had left. I paid for the room in advance with most of the cash I had on me. Using my debit or credit card would be stupid, making it easy for the police to find me. There was only forty dollars left, which meant I would have to resurface in the world sooner than later.

The bi-state bus had been my mode of transportation when I got to the motel. Staying in the slums of the city seemed to be the only sensible move for me at the time. I had to think of a way to get out of town without being seen, but I needed help. I wished again that Lady were here to help me as I thought about her memorial service taking place today. Then again, if the rumors were true she wouldn't have been trustworthy anyway. I thought about what Lucille said and wondered if her words were valid. If drunks didn't do shit else, they spoke the truth when oiled up.

I hopped out of the bed and walked into the bathroom to take a quick shower. There was only so much funk I could take and the poor ass water pressure at the roach motel would have to be enough. I had people to see today, starting with daddy dearest. If he was such a saved man as Tayla claimed him to be, then he would be the perfect person to help me get out of the bullshit I'd created.

* * *

I pulled my hood tighter around my head as I walked through the alley to the backyard of the house I grew up in. Staring at the red brick house brought back a lot of memories that I'd buried to never bring up again but just like herpes, they resurfaced unexpectedly. I shook off the unwanted memories and made my way to the big rock that sat on the back porch. It was where we always kept the spare key. I prayed that the key was still there and just like the predictable man that Michael was known to be, I smiled as the shiny key sat on the ground.

"Guess some things never change," I said to myself as I picked up the key and placed it into the lock.

I opened the door and walked into the kitchen. Nothing had changed inside either. The refrigerator still held some of my childhood pictures, same ugly yellow wallpaper and wooden kitchen table.

I saw myself as a little girl sitting under the table crying and praying that the fighting from the other room would stop and hoping like hell that I wouldn't be the one receiving the drunken ass whooping. I looked away and my eyes landed on the pantry door. There was a tiny hole in the bottom of it that I'd dug out over time. I thought I would be able to make one big enough for me to escape. The closet was my punishment of solitary confinement. He'd taken the light bulb out and would make me sit in there for hours in complete darkness, sometimes days.

I stared up at the ceiling trying not to drop the tears that tugged at my eyes. This house was cancerous for me. Not one good memory in it. It was no wonder I ran from here fast as hell as soon as I was able to.

"Mykah, is that you?" his voice asked softly.

I looked at the door and saw Michael, standing there. Smiling at me as if I would believe this man of God facade he was putting on. When I first heard that he became a minister, I went to one of his services to see it for myself. I sat in a back pew and watched in amazement as Michael ran game over his congregation. I shook my head in disbelief as they eagerly emptied their pockets and gave their last dimes to him. They obviously believed in him, but I saw through his fake ass act. I walked out of there satisfied with the thought that I would never have to see him again but now he stood before me two years later.

He was a lot thinner than I last remembered and his hair was now gray. It wasn't as thick and full but I could still see a wave or two. Even though his caramel brown skin had a yellow tone to it I could still see remnants of the good looking man who drove all the women nuts back in the day. It was clear that he was sick, but he also looked like money was no longer an issue for him. I would bet my entire fortune that his money was why Tayla was with him. There was no other reason for a healthy young woman to be in love with an old piece of shit like Michael. I could see why Tayla thought she had herself a good man. On the outside he appeared to be happy, but I knew the miserable man who lived on the inside.

"Hello, Michael. I heard you've been looking for me."

"I actually didn't think you would come but I'm glad you did." He walked towards me with his arms open for a hug.

I quickly stepped to the side unable to allow myself to accept the love that he was trying to give me. Besides, he wasn't getting off that easy. He hadn't hugged me since I was about five years old and that was only because I'd fallen down a flight of steps and broke my leg. I was in a lot of pain and for once he was able to comfort me.

"I really don't know why the fuck I'm here. I hope you know that I hate you."

He looked at me wearily and pulled out a chair for me to sit down. I didn't sit down though. Instead, I just folded my arms across my chest defiantly. He chuckled slightly and then sat down himself. I walked around to the other side of the table so I could face him. He owed me an explanation.

"I know that you hate me. Hell, I hate myself sometimes, too. When I think about all the things I did to you and your mother, I feel so bad. If I could take it back, I would."

"If? If your grandmother had balls she would be your granddaddy. Ain't that what you used to say to me when I would ask if you loved me? What kind of fucking person says that to a child?"

I yanked the chair out, sat down and stared at him angrily. I was no longer scared of him. He no longer had power when it came to me. I gloated when I saw him shrink down under my glare.

"I've been feeling under the weather for a while now. The doctors can't really figure out what's going on other than my liver is failing me. Hell, I spent years drinking so I'm not surprised it ain't been failed me," Michael chuckled slightly.

I could tell that he was uncomfortable with the fact that he was dying. However, I didn't give a damn about him nor his upcoming death.

"You do look like shit. Hopefully you'll die within the next few seconds so I can be a witness," I replied cruelly.

He shrunk down in his chair after I said that. If he thought this was going to be a pleasant visit, I'd shown that shit was about to get ugly.

"Listen, Mykah, you have to believe me when I say, I'm so sorry. I wasn't in my right frame of mind back then, but I'm a changed man now, I'm saved. That other me was of the world, unhappy, miserable and I took that out on you and your mother. I'm a man of God now. Becoming a minister is the best thing that's ever happened to me. We've all made mistakes. I've actually made a lot of them, but I'm now asking for forgiveness," he stated solemnly.

"Why? Because you were really in love with Lady?"

I threw the question out there and waited for him to tell me that I was tripping. I wanted him to tell me that everything Lucille said was a lie. But when I didn't get a response from him I knew it was true.

"Speaking at her funeral was the hardest thing I've ever done."

Michael loosened his tie as he fought back the tears that were trying to force their way down his face. I'd heard some girls on the bus talking about Lady's funeral today. According to their constant chatter, the hood sent Lady home in grand fashion. I didn't expect them to do anything less. I wished more than anything that I could talk to her one last time. I wanted answers about what happened between her and Michael. Looking at how sad he was, I knew he wouldn't give me what I needed. I couldn't stop the rage that zoomed through me as he sat there in his suit mourning the woman who had helped tear my mother's heart apart. It made me hate him more and surprisingly it made me hate Lady as well. Especially after the shit that Lucille had said about Lady possibly being my real mother.

"Michael, I heard about the little rumor that Lady had a baby by you," I finally blurted out.

His eyes grew to the size of watermelons.

"Supposedly that child died. Or somehow people are saying I may be that child. Tell me that shit is a fucking lie," I screamed at him.

"Mykah, I just, I just don't know what to say," he said with a look of defeat in his eyes.

What Lucille said must have had some sort of truth in it. I could tell by the look on his face.

"Tell me that Lady wasn't my fucking Mama. That's where the hell you should start. It's some crazy shit going on. I need answers as to why you'd allow something like this to happen and then tell me if this has anything to do with why my Mama's dead. Now Lady is dead and I hope you're about to die too. You don't deserve to live either. Michael!" I continued to scream and berate him.

He calmly reached across the table and grabbed my hands. He tried to steady my nerves, but the rage I felt inside continued to make my entire body shake. I snatched my hands away from him and shoved them inside the pocket of my hoody. I didn't want him touching me. It was bad enough we shared the same blood and if I could remove that from my veins without dying I would have.

"Mykah I can't change the past, baby girl, but I'm gonna try and right the future. It doesn't matter who your real mother is because they both loved you. And I do too. I hate that I missed out on your life but I promise to right all of my wrongs starting now. Hell, I don't even know your girls. I used to go by their school every day and watch Jamison take them home, but haven't felt up to it these days. They're really beautiful. Do you know if they're okay?"

"So, you've been telling everybody around town for me to call you just for you to tell me that you're a stalker?"

"Um no, I just wanted to see you and apologize. Let me help you. I heard about what happened with you running your car into theirs." He paused and looked at me as if I had major issues. "The police have been by looking for you. You need to get out of town as soon as possible, and I can help you with that."

I looked at him in surprise. I don't know why because the police reaching out to my family wasn't that far-fetched. It made perfect sense because family was who people turned to in their time of need. He must have really felt like shit in order to risk going to jail for helping me.

"Do you know what I do for a living?" I asked him.

His eyes never connected with mine. They darted all around the room. He moved around in his chair trying to find a comfortable position. He was now nervous. He cleared his throat several times before speaking.

"Tayla hasn't gone into details but it's something that she prays about a lot. For your safety and for God to change your heart," he said so softly that I had to strain to hear him.

"What if I told you I kill men for a living, let's say hypothetically?"

He didn't say anything. He just stared at me with the saddest pair of eyes ever. This time his sadness was not about Lady. It was because he knew that he fucked me up and no matter how much he pretended to be a different person, I was still fucked up because of his sins.

"It's cool, you don't have to answer because I'm going to tell you whether you want to hear it or not. I kill men because each time I take their worthless, good for nothing ass lives, I wish it was you. In that last moment, right before they take their last breaths, I wish it was your ass that I was killing. All those nights, I cried and prayed that someone would hear me and come save me, but no one came. Mama was so caught up on your ass that even with two black eyes and a bruised lip, she would defend her love for you. You took her power and mine too by making us your punching bags."

His tears fell and even that seemed to anger me even more. I didn't want this pitiful ass man to give in so easy. I needed my fight with him. I needed to let him know that I could finally stand my ground with him.

"Mykah, really, I swear I'm so," he started to say.

"Sorry. I get it now. You really are a sorry ass excuse for a man. I don't see how I was so scared of you because actually you're weak as fuck. I should kill your ass right now," I said pulling out the gun that I'd bought off a kid on the street with the last thirty dollars I had.

My hand shook and I tried to take deep breaths to calm my nerves. The moment had finally come, it was time to put an end to my miserable ass childhood memories. The invisible scars that I wore would disappear as soon as I put an end to him. He held his hands up and started to chant some sort of prayer. I couldn't quite process his words because I was too busy looking at the band on his ring finger. I hadn't heard that he'd gotten married. And it wasn't the ring that he wore when my mom was alive. He'd pawned that a long time ago.

"What the hell is that?" I asked him while nodding to his hand.

"This is part of the reason I wanted to talk to you so bad. I recently got married. Just put the gun down so we can talk," he replied cautiously.

I readjusted my hold on the gun and shook my head at him. I didn't know what planet he was living on, but from where I stood, we wouldn't be negotiating a damn thing.

"I'm running this so don't tell me what to do. I knew you were the same ole shiesty ass piece of shit that you've always been. You have Tayla running around here quoting that gibberish you've been speaking. She thinks she's in love with you but you're fucking married. Wow!"

This would devastate Tayla when she found out. For the past few months she had built her whole life around her great mystery man that turned out to be Michael and he was married to another woman.

"I know he's married, Mykah. He's married to me," Tayla said while walking slowly into the kitchen.

My eyes increased. "What? I'm sorry. Bitch, what did you just say? You married Michael." I looked down at Tayla's left hand, eyeing the simple gold band she wore. It was piece of jewelry that she'd obviously been hiding for a while.

I shook my head back and forth as if I'd suddenly gone crazy. I felt sick to my stomach at the thought of Tayla actually marrying him. Tayla actually being my stepmother. This shit just had to be some sort of sick ass joke.

"We've been trying to think of a good way to tell you. I knew it wouldn't be easy, but if you just see him as the man that I do, you will understand that he has genuinely changed, Mykah," Tayla tried to explain.

"I don't believe what the hell I'm hearing. It's like I'm in the fucking twilight zone. You can't possibly be married to him. I refuse to believe you're that damn dumb!" I yelled at her.

"I'm not dumb but I am in love," Tayla tried to assure me.

"No way, I'm going to need some proof of that. I know you and I know the only thing that you love is money? So...did Michael promise you that he would give you money out of the collection plate or something?" It looked like Tayla wanted to slap the shit out of me as I continued. "I mean he's on the brink of damn death so I'm guessing there's some sort of life insurance policy and you're the beneficiary, right?"

"I'm sorry, Mykah, but I love him; he's my husband. I hope you can respect that and move on. This has nothing to do with money and everything to do with love. So again, I say respect our relationship."

"Respect that? Are you fucking kidding me? We used to plan his murder together when we were little and now you're his wife. You don't see shit clearly anymore. You don't just move on when the person who was supposed to protect you was the one causing you harm," I said through tears.

My hand continued to shake as Tayla walked closer to me. She stood at my side. I shifted my weight in the chair to make sure that she wouldn't try to take the gun from me. I pointed it back and forth between her and Michael. He looked like he was two seconds from passing out, but Tayla stood steadfast with a relaxed look on her face.

"So you kill me and him, then what? That's not gonna help you get Jamison back," she said.

She was right. Killing the two of them would never bring Jamison back, and it was the one thing I wished I could change. He was a good man and he didn't deserve to die all because I was incapable of loving him properly.

"I didn't mean to kill Jamison. I swear I didn't," I cried.

"Jamison didn't die, Mykah. He's at Barnes Hospital in a coma, but he's still holding on."

I looked at Tayla trying to see if she was lying, but there was no indication of deceit in her eyes.

"I saw him, Tayla. He was slumped over and bleeding. He wasn't moving. I saw him! Jamison died!" I yelled. "They even posted his picture in the news and it said DEATH AT A LOCAL SCHOOL."

"No, he didn't die. I wouldn't lie to you about this."

"Don't fucking lie to me just so I won't kill his ass. Jamison is dead!"

I pointed the gun at her this time. She threw her hands up but continued to try and reason with me.

"I saw him earlier, Mykah. This has nothing to do with us. Jamison is alive."

A heavy weight immediately was lifted off my shoulders. For the first time since running into his car I smiled. There was finally a rainbow at the end of this storm I was in.

"Jamison is alive? Oh my God, I'm so happy. I thought I'd killed him. Tayla, I have to go see him and make it right. Where are the girls? Have you seen them?" I rambled crazily as I lowered the gun.

When water began to fill Tayla's eyes, I knew that she was about to tell me something that would turn everything dark again.

"Mykah, I swear I'm sorry to have to tell you this but..." She paused for a few seconds.

"But what? Spit it out!"

"Umm Malia she umm, Malia died."

"What? What do you mean, Malia died? Where's Jasmine?"

"When you hit the car, you hit the front and the back, damaging the entire driver's side. There was some internal bleeding in her liver that wasn't diagnosed because Malia was pegged to make it at first. She was up walking around and talking, and we really thought she was good."

"No. Shut up, Tayla. Shut the fuck up!" I screamed.

I grabbed the table to keep myself from falling out of the chair. I started humming to myself trying to block out what Tayla was telling me. She didn't know what she was talking about. Jamison was the one who died, there was no way it could have been Malia.

"She fainted in the waiting room while Jamison was in surgery. Doctors did all they could, but there was no saving her," Tayla said through tears.

"No, you're lying. It's not fucking true, I don't believe you." I stood up.

"Mykah, please just sit back down. Let me get you some water or something," Michael said.

"No, no I don't believe it. I gotta get the fuck out of here!"

"She's dead, Mykah. You killed Malia. You need to fucking deal with it," Tayla grabbed me and screamed in my face.

I shook my head back in forth in disbelief. Michael reached out to hold me but I smacked his hands away from me. I didn't need his comfort. This was all his fault. I grabbed the gun and pointed it at him. If the wages of sin was death, today was his judgment day.

"I love you," he said with a slight smile on his face.

"Fuck you," I said before pulling the trigger.

Chapter 18

I sat in the car staring at my reflection in the rear view mirror. I looked like shit. I was so close to actually killing Michael when Tayla told me what I'd done to Malia. As bad as I wanted to shoot him in his heart, I shot the damn pantry door instead and then shot up anything I could, destroying Michael's prized possessions. It gave me some sort of relief, but now an hour later my mind was still on Malia.

Even though Michael beat my ass and tortured me on a daily, he didn't take my life. I'd killed Malia so that actually made me worse than him. After learning the news, Michael and Tayla desperately tried to console me, but there was no use. I didn't need their comfort. What I needed was his car so I could execute my escape without getting caught. Michael hadn't been good for shit for as long as I could remember, but he had actually come through for me giving me the keys to his Tahoe along with five hundred dollars. I was shocked, but it still didn't right all the pain he caused. It was his fault that I was put in the situation and that ultimately resulted in the death of my child. I felt so sick to my stomach I could barely sit up straight and drive.

They both tried to talk me into staying the night, but I was getting on the first thing smoking out of St. Louis. I wasn't sure how I would do that knowing that the police probably had my picture posted up everywhere. Even with the money that Michael was able to give me, I needed to get my hands on a large sum of money, and I knew the only way I could do that was to withdraw the money from my secret account. Thankfully, Lady had me put the account under a fake name and ID she'd given me. So there was no way the police would be able to track this account to me.

I looked in the mirror again and adjusted the spiral curled black wig that Tayla gave me. On the ID the wig was longer, but I still looked the same. I wiped the tears from my face and poured some drops in my eyes, trying to kill some of the redness from them.

Satisfied with my appearance, I got out of the car and strolled into the bank. I didn't bother filling out a withdrawal slip. Instead, I walked straight to the office of my personal banker. I was going to withdraw the money and give Tayla half of it to give to Jasmine. With me on the run, Jamison in a coma and Malia dead, she was gonna need as much help as possible. It was killing me not being able to call her and explain that I never meant for any of this to happen. Despite our differences, she was still my daughter and I loved her. The last thing I wanted was for Jasmine to think I'd killed her sister intentionally. I wanted her to know that it was just an accident.

"Excuse me, is Mark Perry here?" I asked the young white man sitting at his desk.

"Mark is currently out sick for a while so I've taken over some of his accounts. My name is Jacob Smith. It's a pleasure to meet you. Is there something I can assist you with?" he asked with a smile plastered on his face.

I'd only dealt with Mark at the bank since I opened my account. I didn't recognize this freckled face man, but I would do whatever I had to do in order to get my money in a hurry so I could leave. I smiled and took a seat across from him. He looked at his watch and then back at me. I guess I was taking too long to spit out what I wanted.

"I'm sorry to hear about Mark. He's been my personal banker for a very long time, but unfortunately I'm moving out of town and I want to withdraw my funds from the bank. You can just put it in a cashier's check."

"And your name is?"

"Dominique Beckley," I told him while handing him my ID.

"Okay, Ms. Beckley, I'm going to need you to fill out a withdrawal slip and I'll be more than happy to assist you."

Jacob picked up the ID while typing my information into the computer. He shifted uncomfortably in his seat a few times and cleared his throat. I became nervous while watching him. I pressed my fingers against the pounding in my temples that rapidly grew with each passing second.

"Umm, Ms. Beckley, there seems to be a bit of confusion. It looks like your money was withdrawn yesterday," he said to me.

I might have been imagining things, but it felt like time had stopped. His lips continued to move but I heard none of his words. The only sound I could hear was the ringing in my eardrums and myself constantly saying that my money was gone.

"Ms. Beckley, hello Ms. Beckley," Jacob said louder finally pulling me from my stupor.

"I'm sitting here right now asking for my money so how could you possibly have given it to me yesterday?"

He shook his head. "I don't know what's going on, but it looks as if my supervisor signed off on this transaction yesterday."

He shifted around in his seat again. I stared at him trying to decide if I should jump over the desk and choke his ass out, or just go all the way postal and set it off. I knew that neither decision would be wise because that would have the police in the bank quick as hell. I took a deep breath, counted to ten and then spoke to him again. The sixth sense in my belly told me that he was about to ruin my chances of going on the run.

"Are you telling me that someone who looked like me came in here and you let them walk away with 1.5 million damn dollars? Please tell me that's not what the fuck you're telling me!" I yelled at him despite trying to keep my cool.

"Ms. Beckley I'm going to need you to calm down. I'm going to talk to my supervisor and find out what happened. I just need for you to stay calm so the guards don't think it's a problem in here."

He nodded toward the see thru glass. I followed his gaze to the faces of the guards and the other employees. They all were staring into the office at the commotion I caused. His face was bright red as he loosened the bright red tie around his scrawny neck. The sweat that poured down his face, left his carrot top hair wet on his forehead.

"Listen, I really don't give a damn about any of that. All I want is my damn money," I said through clenched teeth.

"I understand this may be difficult for you but trust me, I'm going to get to the bottom of it."

The headache that immediately exploded inside of my head was so intense I rubbed my temples, attempting to get some sort of relief. I was two seconds from choking the shit out of Jacob and couldn't control the rage inside of me. I took a deep breath and looked up.

"You haven't even begun to see difficult yet. I'm sitting here now broke as hell and someone out there is sitting on a shit load of my money. I suggest you go and get your fucking supervisor before things get real difficult for your ass."

Jacob hurriedly stood and grabbed my file from his cabinet. He walked down the hall to his supervisor's office. I looked through the glass window at the heated exchange that the two shared. Jacob's head hung low like a scorned child. I could tell that whatever news he came back with wouldn't work in my favor.

He and the supervisor walked back towards me with tight lips. That was white people code for some deep shit had gone down and they were left perplexed about it.

"Hi, Ms. Beckley. I'm Diane Summers, the bank supervisor, I was told that you have a bit of a misunderstanding about some funds you withdrew," the fat female supervisor said to me.

I looked her up and down. She reminded me of Rikki Lake back when she was fat. Her chubby cheeks were redder than they normally were. Whenever I came into the bank she walked around as if she had no other life outside of the bank. We never really had any personal interaction with one another other than a smile and a head nod. It always seemed like she loved her job a little too much and mishandling of a large sum of money like mine was something she didn't want to happen on her watch.

"There's no fucking misunderstanding here! It seems like you and your employee gave my damn money away! But here is where you come in at, you're going to go back there and talk this shit over with your insurance company and tell them that your former employee, Jacob, made a huge ass mistake, and they're going to tell you to give me my damn money and then everyone will be happy."

"I actually signed off on the transaction. A large amount of money like that being withdrawn has to go through a supervisor first. I checked all the necessary documents. You did withdraw your money yesterday," Diane said firmly, while handing me the withdrawal slip.

I let out a nervous laugh. "I'm trying to remain calm here but you lost my fucking money and that's a big problem for me. I don't have much time so I'm going to sit here for five more minutes and wait for you to come back with my check," I hissed.

"Listen, I don't want any problems. We've never had a situation like this. I pulled the security clearance from yesterday and you did indeed withdraw your funds. If you would like to come into my office, I can show you," Diane said while walking towards the door.

I nodded my head and we all walked the short trip to Diane's office. We huddled around her desk and I couldn't help but notice that she had several pictures of cats all over it. She sat down and immediately started typing. After she got into the program, Diane turned her monitor around so that Jacob and I could see.

We watched and waited for whoever the slick bitch was that had my money. The tape seemed to take forever, but somewhere around 12:00 p.m. a woman walked in. She looked exactly like me. I watched the way she moved and noticed that she had me down to the very last sway. Her black wig sat on her head and a mole was under her left eyes. My mouth dropped open when she paused the tape and zoomed in on the woman.

It was Malia! She was dressed in all black and leather, and actually reminded me of Jasmine because Malia would never be caught in such dark colors. I would've thought it was Jasmine, but she dressed more tomboyish and the person on the screen was dressed sexy in skintight clothing.

To anyone else, especially those who believed Malia was dead would've thought it was Jasmine, but I knew the two apart. I birthed them. A mother knows who her kids are regardless of how good or bad she is to them. I was so happy to see her alive that I wanted to scream out loud. The bank reps all looked at me and then back at the screen. They couldn't tell us apart. I tried to regain my composure but it was a struggle. Seeing Malia on that screen trying to be me brought up a lot of questions and emotions. I needed to process the information but I couldn't do it in the bank.

It felt like I was about to pass out as I rubbed my throbbing temples once again. All of my fucking money was gone!

"I'm sorry, I haven't been feeling like myself lately. I recently fell and bumped my head. I'm sorry to have wasted your time," I said while standing.

Diane and Jacob both hit me with sympathetic smiles. Diane looked more relieved than anything. She hadn't made a mistake so she was all good, but I was just fucked out of everything I'd worked so hard for, risked my life for and ruined my family for. Malia had stolen my money. My daughter who Tayla told me had died.

Why would she lie to me? Why was Malia trying to act like Jasmine? Where was Jasmine? What the fuck is going on? How the hell does Malia know about my secret account? All of these thoughts spun around in my head like tumbleweed as I quickly made my way out of the bank.

I sat in the car in the parking lot unable to breathe. I had no way to get out of town without any money.

I needed that money! I'd worked too hard for it.

The rage I felt inside caused my entire body to tremble. I took a deep breath to stop my shaking hands as I grabbed Michael's cell phone that I swiped off of the table and dialed Malia's cell number.

"What?" She answered angrily.

"I don't know what the fuck is going on but I know you got my money and I want that shit back. Where are you?"

"Well if it ain't the psycho ass mother who killed her own child and almost murdered her husband."

"I don't know what you up to Malia but I'm serious when I say, I want my damn money back. Where the fuck are you?"

"Why don't you meet me at the police station and I'll give you your money. I hear they looking for you," she responded sarcastically.

"This ain't a game, Malia."

"I never intended for it to be, you made it that way. You killed my sister and for that, you are going to pay worse than what we originally intended for you."

"Who the hell is, we?" I asked her in surprise.

First Kip said we and now Malia. Whoever the fuck we was, they were all about to see the very bad side of me.

"Don't rush your death, Mother. That shit will happen when I say it's time. Until then, you bore me so goodbye," she said before hanging up.

I quickly dialed her back but the call rolled over to voicemail. I sat in the car unable to breathe. I let the window down assuming that would give me some relief but I felt a panic attack coming on. I had no way to get out of town without any money. I needed that damn money. It was mine and I was going to do everything to make sure I could get that back.

As much as I hated to do it, I picked up the cellphone again and dialed the only person who could help me at this point.

The phone rang several times before he finally answered.

"Hello, Dyson? I need you."

Chapter 19

"Dyson, are you here?" I asked while walked into the dark living room.

When I called him from the bank, he told me to come to his loft so we could talk. I hadn't answered any of his calls since that night I left him shooting up. I was sure he had plenty of questions to ask me. I had questions for him too. The first one being, why he'd put a hit out on Lady. I really thought he was a good person. I also thought I had a natural gift for judging a person's character. I couldn't have been more wrong. Lady, Jamison, Dyson, Tayla and even my own daughters had all betrayed me in one way or another.

Dyson where are you?" I yelled a little louder this time.

I flipped the light switch on the wall but nothing happened. I then walked over to the lamp on the end table, but still there was no power. I pulled the cell phone out of my pocket and used the light from the screen to guide myself around the apartment. The light was only bright enough to illuminate a few feet in front of me as I held onto the wall walking into the back of the house.

"Dyson, are you okay? Where are you?"

I knocked on the bathroom door thinking he could've been inside, but it was empty. As I walked back towards the living room, suddenly I could smell the faint smell of cigarette smoke. It wasn't there when I first walked in so that instantly put me on alert. I put the cell phone down and felt around for the gun on my side only to realize that I'd left it in the car. I paused trying to think of what kind of weapon I could use out of Dyson's household objects, but being in the hallway limited me. I tried to steady my breathing but I was nervous that I'd been caught slipping.

"Come on in, Mykah. We have some shit to discuss," the voice said into the still air.

I didn't have to see her face to know that it was Chauntelle. I did slightly wonder how she knew that I was here. The thought of her being back with Dyson made me cringe. I stepped into the room and looked at the cigarette that lit up each time she took a puff. She was sitting straight up, posted up as if she ran the fucking place. She had a flashlight in her hand and wasted no time flicking the light in my face. I covered my eyes trying to adjust to the sudden change of scenery.

"What the fuck do you want Chauntelle?"

"I'm trying to see if I want to call the police and let them come take you away or do I want to deal with you myself. Decisions, decisions. What's a girl to do?" She twirled the flashlight in her hand and laughed at her own little joke. I was pissed at myself for getting into this situation. I should've known that I couldn't trust Dyson.

"Why are you here? What are you looking for and where the fuck is Dyson?"

"I'm looking for my damn money. I told you when I first met you that I don't let people play with my money. Since you obviously didn't handle your business, I want a fucking refund immediately. As far as Dyson is concerned, he's not your concern, sweetie," Chauntelle responded.

We stared at each other for a moment. My thoughts were all over the place. Since I couldn't find my center, I had no way of processing how I would be the one to walk out of this room alive. Chauntelle was small but she seemed to thrive off her hatred for me. I wasn't sure what she was thinking, but from the smirk that tugged at her lips, I knew that it was something twisted.

"Where is Dyson?"

Chauntelle tossed her head back and let out a big hearty laugh. She then put the cigarette butt out on the edge of the table and sat back in the plush leather chair.

"Your fucking husband is in the hospital and your daughter is dead and you have the nerve to ask me about my husband? Wow, you really are a fucked up person, Mykah. I can totally see why Jamison turned to me in his time of need. Just for the record, we didn't plan to hook up. That just happened out of his loneliness. I saw him come up to that school for every event, no matter what it was. I realized that I wanted a man like that in my life. I had everything a girl could want with Dyson, materialistically speaking but there was no love there. Not like what Jamison had for you. I wanted that. Just like with everything else, I got him."

Her mentioning Jamison caused my hand to twitch. And I wondered if she knew Malia wasn't really dead. Tears welled up in my eyes from just hearing her speak of my family. I wanted to beat their names from her mouth. I walked closer towards Chauntelle trying to intimidate her, but she didn't coward down. In fact, she picked up a .45 that she had sitting on her lap and pointed it at me. I immediately stopped in my tracks. Even though I was now nervous because I didn't have my gun on me, I didn't want to let her see it.

"If you say their names again, I swear I'll fuck you up," I warned her.

"Wow, what a performance. You almost made me think that you actually give a fuck. You probably should've been an actress," she said condescendingly.

"Not that I have to explain anything to you but I do love my family and I'll kill anyone who fucks with them."

"You love them so much that you rammed into Jamison's car with your kids in it? That's not love, bitch. Not love at all."

That comment hurt. Punched me in my gut with a Mike Tyson kind of blow. I felt sick just thinking about how true her statement was.

Keep your cool, she has a gun. I told myself before responding. "Mind your fucking business before I mind it for you."

"You don't scare me, Mykah. I don't see how you are able to kill so many people because you remind me of a soft pussy. All wet and mushy, easy to stretch in any position it's put in. Lady should've recruited me instead of you."

"Lady should have recruited you? What the fuck are you talking about?" I questioned.

"Oh, you didn't know that little piece of information, huh? Just like you, Lady and me go way back. You think she would be that involved with Dyson and I would've never met her. Damn, Mykah, you really aren't that bright."

"I don't give a fuck about what you're talking about," I lied.

Truth was I wrecked my brain trying to figure out what the hell was going on. When I went to Lady with the information about Chauntelle she never said anything about knowing her personally, only what she'd heard about her. I was now more confused than ever as I realized Lady wasn't the person I thought she was.

"Oh you should care because your little world is about to come tumbling down and I'm going to be the one who breaks it. Well, me and some other people. But before that happens, I want my money back."

"I have to go to the bank," I said, lying again.

Hell, that was my first blow of the day, realizing that Malia stole my money. As soon as I finished with this Chauntelle shit, I was going to find a way to get my hands on Malia's ass.

"Try again. I already know that shit is bone dry at the bank. So, once more, I'll ask you where is my fucking money?" She cocked the gun back.

Hearing the clicking sound, I knew that if I didn't make a move sooner versus later, she wouldn't hesitate to shoot me. I needed to somehow get her to loosen up a little bit, throw her off her game for just a second so that I could make a power move. I put my hands up and backed up into the chair on the opposite side of her. I thought she would assume that I'd given up if I sat down and seemed vulnerable.

"I knew when I first met you that I would enjoy putting a bullet in your smug ass. You thought that shit was funny when you made me strip down. Now look who's about to get the last laugh. Strip, bitch!" she yelled at me.

"Listen, Chauntelle. We both know that Malia is alive and she stole my money. We can work together to get it back from her and then we can split it 50/50," I blurted out.

There was no way I was about to strip down. We would have to fight this shit out until there was only one of us left standing.

"Malia still alive? That can't be right. They told me she died," Chauntelle mumbled.

"Who the fuck is this *they* and *we* you keep talking about? Looks like whoever they are, they didn't tell you all of their plans. You must be at the bottom of the fucking chain," I said trying to piss her off.

I watched the look of confusion wash over her face as she seemed to be in deep thought. I didn't have a clue what her crazy ass was talking about, but I took that as my moment to react. I hopped out of the chair and rushed her. We both fell onto the polished hardwood floor. The sudden impact caused Chauntelle to lose control of the gun. She tried to feel around for it, but I grabbed her hair forcefully and quickly landed two jabs to her face. I hit her with the same punch that I gave Lucille, but Chauntelle was a lot tougher than her. Her fingers clawed at my face, drawing blood on both side of my cheeks.

"Fuck!" I yelled.

I tried to punch her again, but she was able to flip us over. Chauntelle grabbed my hair and banged my head against the floor. I winced from pain, but I was determined to beat her ass. She'd shaken my world up from the first moment I saw her. Within seconds, I grabbed her throat and tried to squeeze out every fucking lie she'd ever told out of it. But the harder I squeezed, the more she laughed.

"This is like foreplay, bitch. You gotta come harder than this," she managed to get out.

When her long nails dug into my wrist, I had no choice but to let her go. I never got a chance to protect myself before Chauntelle punched me in the face with a force so powerful it knocked the wind out of me. I heard the bone crack in my nose instantly. The pain, although unbearable, didn't stop me from wanting to kill her. I attempted to get a hold of her hair or shirt. I needed to stop her quick movements, but she smacked my hands away, dodging me. I'd definitely underestimated her power. She was a lot stronger than the prissy princess I pegged her to be. There was definitely some hood pumping through her blood mixed with a dose of pure evil. I'd shot men ten times bigger than her, but actual fighting turned out to be a greater struggle.

Chauntelle got on her knees. While pulling my hair with her right hand, she used the left one to feel around on the floor for the gun. I closed my eyes and decided to take the excruciating pain of both my nose and hair being pulled as Chauntelle held on for dear life.

She continued to drag me around the floor, searching in the dark room for her gun. As Chauntelle stuffed her hand in the bottom of the couch, just that temporary shift allowed me to maneuver my hair out of her hand. I quickly raised up on my knees and threw all my body weight on top of her. We fell against the couch, tumbling back on the floor.

Our hands hit the gun at the same time and it became a new struggle to see who was going to gain control of it. I was tired and she was breathing heavily. Her cigarette smoke filled lungs was no match for my endurance. I had the majority of the gun in my hand when I turned it towards Chauntelle.

"I told you I would come out on top, bitch," I bragged to her.

She stopped wrestling and looked at me with wide eyes. I was glad that my face would be the last one embedded in her head.

"You lose bitch. Tell Kip I said hello when you get to hell."

I pulled the trigger and waited to see death creep slowly over her. For one second I thought it was over, but nothing came out of the gun.

"You gotta be fucking kidding me," I said, realizing the gun had jammed.

At that moment, Chauntelle head butted me like some shit you see in the movies, causing me to fall off of her body. We both were sort of dazed from the blow and neither of us could move for a few seconds. I stood up first trying to gain my composure. I shook my head several times. I wanted to charge her again, but my mind was still in a haze.

"You have to be the worst assassin ever. You couldn't even kill Dyson and you had him served up on a fucking platter for you. I don't know what Lady saw in your ass and sure don't understand what Dyson saw," she said while standing as well.

The gun was now in her hand. I watched her every move as she wiped the blood from her nose and spit out the blood in her mouth. I hoped like hell that gun was still jammed as Chauntelle cocked the gun back.

"You should've sent me on my way that morning I came into your fake ass place of business. You almost did, but greed got the best of you. Kip said it would. He knew immediately that you were a thirsty whore for money. Dyson should've listened to him. Your life would have been so much easier if you didn't set this chess game in motion. They planned to destroy you from the jump," Chauntelle informed.

"I don't even know what the fuck you're talking about. What chess game? Who planned to destroy me?" I asked her.

"I think it would be better if you die not knowing what was in front of your face all along. Is there anything you want me to tell Jamison or Dyson for you?" she asked me.

"Go to hell, bitch," I spat at her.

If I was about to die, I for damn sure wasn't about to beg for my life. I didn't have any words for her to give anyone. It was obvious that trusting Lady and Dyson had gotten me nothing.

"How about you go to hell first and make sure the place is ready for me?" she responded.

I closed my eyes unable to look at the bullet as it traveled towards me. The loud popping sound rang in my ears. My body jerked. It seemed to take forever for the bullet to hit me, and for my body to hit the floor. All I could think of was how I'd chosen money over family. I'd failed them and would never have a chance to make it up to them.

Chapter 20

"Get up, Mykah. You haven't been shot," Dyson said while walking in the living room from the back of the apartment.

I opened my eyes and immediately began to feel around on my chest and stomach in total disbelief that I wasn't dead. I hopped up and quickly took notice that the lights were back on. Chauntelle was lying on the floor in a pool of blood. She'd been shot in the chest. Dyson kicked her gun away from her, then leaned over her and checked her pulse.

"Crazy ass, bitch," he spewed at her dead body.

Dyson turned towards me with the gun still in his hand and his finger still on the trigger. I immediately backed away, scurrying across the floor, trying to find somewhere safe to run. He seemed upset that I didn't trust him.

"Mykah, I'm not going to hurt you. That bitch, Chauntelle knocked me out while I was in the room taking my insulin. She snuck up behind me. She turned off the circuit breaker, that's why it was so dark. I don't know how or when she got in here," he said while putting the gun down.

"Insulin?" I questioned.

I looked around the room as I tried to process the fact that it was Chauntelle and not me lying on that floor. Somehow the universe was on my side and I was still alive.

"Yeah, insulin. It's not something that I just run around telling everyone but I'm diabetic. We need to get out of here though. We'll have plenty of time to talk about that shit in the car."

"So you're not on drugs?"

"Hell no."

I thought I saw you shooting up the night Kip came over here."

I walked in circles as I thought back to that night. I didn't actually see what Dyson did, but I did see the needle and I panicked thinking it was drugs. I felt stupid for assuming the worse about him.

"Is that why you left and wasn't taking my calls? You thought that little of me? A fucking junkie? Look, we gotta get the fuck outta here now," Dyson said while shaking his head at me.

I looked up at him still trying to process all that just happened. He wasn't a junkie but he did have Lady killed. I couldn't trust that he wouldn't do the same to me. I didn't want to go anywhere with him, but I had to play along since he was the one holding the gun.

"How are we going to get rid of her? There's way too much blood to clean this up."

I looked down at Chauntelle and shuddered at the way the bullet tore through her once beautiful face. Her gray eyes were still open and held the look of shock in them. Even in death they were piercingly spooky.

"Fuck her. I'll have my boys come get this together. Let's go," Dyson ordered.

"So, you're just gonna leave her here like this? What if the police come? That gun shot was loud."

"Are you okay, Mykah? Did she hurt you?" he asked, ignoring my questions.

He allowed his forefinger to trace the side of my face softly. It was crazy how this man made me feel. My panties moistened at the thought of him touching me. It was crazy how you could fear a man, but want him all at the same time.

"No, I'm okay. I think my nose may be broken, but other than that I'm good. What about you?"

I tried to make it seem like I wasn't in a great deal of pain, but I was seconds from passing out from the thumping in my head. I held it with my right hand and tried to gently massage my now swollen nose with my other hand. Dyson went in the kitchen and grabbed a towel and some ice. I still seemed somewhat apprehensive about his presence as he placed the towel gently on my nose.

"Look, we don't have a lot of time to get out of here. Shit is about to get real so we need to bounce right now. I've been calling you like crazy. They got you splashed all over the fucking news for killing your kid and shit. What the fuck is going on with you?"

In my daze, I'd completely forgotten about that problem. I had no way to get the information I needed in regards to Jamison's health and what was going on with Jasmine and Malia. I knew for a fact that Malia was alive because she stole my money, but I didn't know if Jasmine was okay. I couldn't stop myself from crying. When Dyson walked towards me again, this time I allowed him to hold me in his arms. I was hurt and confused about all of this shit that happened over the past few weeks. How had I fallen so fast? I pulled away from him and looked him in his eyes.

"So much shit has happened that I don't even know where to begin. Everything and everyone that I thought I knew, I don't. Starting with Lady on down to my husband and kids. I'm confused as hell and don't know how to make any of this right. I wish I could take it all back," I cried.

The hot, salty tears burned the fresh cuts and scratches on my face. I took the pain as some form of atonement.

"Damn, Mykah. It'll be okay. We'll figure it out, but for now we gotta get out of here. The police are looking for you and umm I heard earlier there's a bounty out for you."

I stopped crying and looked up at him in shock. *Who in the hell would possibly put a bounty out on me*, I thought. "What do you mean there's a bounty on me? Who ordered it?" I asked.

Dyson looked at me as if he was trying to decide how much information I could handle for one night. I thought about the last time he placed an order on someone's life. We were in this same apartment when he told Kip to kill Lady. Just thinking about it made me mad all over again.

"Let's just go. I'll explain it to you in the car," he said while pulling my arm towards him again.

I yanked out of his reach and placed my hands on my hips. I wanted some fucking answers and Dyson would be giving me those before I took another step.

"Why did you have Lady killed?" I blurted out.

The question stopped him from moving. His eyes watered a little and he looked away from me.

"Look, I don't really feel like getting into that right now. That's not some shit I wanted to agree to, but you don't say no to Preston LaRue, not if you want to keep living yourself. He thought it looked weak that we let her grandson go without punishment after he stole money from us. She vouched for him and it cost her life. I loved Lady. I even paid to bury her, every single thing down to the smallest flower was paid for by me. She was set on fire, straight had to be cremated. She didn't deserve that. She made me who I am, but he made me do it. I didn't have a choice," he mumbled.

"What do you mean, he made you do it? Don't fucking play me like I'm stupid, you did it because you wanted to. I heard you tell Kip to do that shit!" I yelled. I was tired of everyone's bullshit.

"I told you I didn't have a fucking choice! It was her or me and don't think Preston wouldn't have me killed because I'm his son," he screamed back at me, "he's done it before."

What had I gotten myself into? Preston LaRue was insane and deadly.

Dyson paced the floor like he was in pain but I didn't give a damn about any of that. I was angry hearing the details of how Lady was murdered. Burning in a fire was a horrible way to die.

"You fucking asshole. You damn right she didn't deserve that shit. I should've killed your ass!" I screamed uncontrollably.

He looked at me incredulously. As his nose flared, the real Dyson LaRue quickly washed over his face. The evil Dyson that I'd heard so much about was now in the room.

Looking at him instantly calmed me down. He looked demented.

"You should've killed me, huh? Well, why didn't you? Was it the dick? Money? What, tell me what the fuck made me so special that you didn't do me like you did all those other niggas."

I knew that my secret was out. It was written all over his face that he knew I was sent for him. I didn't know what to say. I didn't know what would trigger him to make him madder so shutting up seemed like my best option.

"So, now your ass wants to be silent and shit, huh? Why the fuck you ain't talking now, Mykah?"

As we stared at each other, I thought about what I could say to bring his temper down a few notches. I didn't want this to escalate into anything further. He knew that I was supposed to kill him and I was scared that he would now kill me.

"How long have you known?" I asked him quietly.

"I knew right after you left my club that night. You know I don't fuck with too many people. That's how I knew where you worked and how to find you. Kip told me that you were hired to kill me. He said Lady had you do it."

I thought about Kip's gorilla looking ass and I'd never been happier that I killed him. He was a snake motherfucker who meant Dyson no good. It happened all the time, the lieutenant was tired of being second in hand. He was jealous of Dyson and knew how much his influence meant so he used that to his advantage.

"Actually, Kip lied to you. It was Chauntelle who hired me and I believe he knew it was her. She offered me half a million dollars to kill you, but I could never bring myself to do it. At first I was just turned on whenever I was around you, but now I think I love you."

"You *think* you love me?" Dyson questioned.

He put heavy emphasis on the word think. It seemed to piss him off. He glared into my face confirming that he felt the same way about me.

"You were sent to fucking kill me but I just killed my wife because she was about to smoke you. Now, I'm about to go to war to protect you from some shit that's about to go down and you say you *think* you love me? Well, I know I fucking love you. My actions show that shit too, so let's fucking go!"he yelled.

"Okay, Dyson. I'm sorry. I do love you. Everything is just so confusing for me right now. I'm going through a lot of shit. Don't you see that?"

Once again I had tears falling down my face. This entire situation had turned me from the cold, heartless bitch to a weak ass cry baby.

"If you love me then listen to what the fuck I'm trying to tell you. We need to get the fuck outta here," he said while pulling me towards the front door again.

When Dyson stopped at his security monitor, a look of horror washed over his face. I looked at the screen and saw two men with black ski masks walking in the lobby. It was only 6:00 p.m. and hot as hell for even a May day. If the masks were on their faces it wasn't to protect them from the cold. It could only mean one thing. I knew that it wasn't good for us.

"Look, Mykah. The real shit is about to go down now. If you as good as I heard you are, you can handle your own, but I want you to follow my lead."

"I don't need to follow your lead, Dyson. I can han…" I attempted to state my independence, but Dyson cut me off.

"Damnit, Mykah. Shut the fuck up and get to the spare bedroom. We can go down the fire escape. It'll let us out around back where my garage is. You need to drive just in case I need to shoot a motherfucker."

The tone of his voice straightened me up and I did as I was told. We raced to the bedroom and just as we cleared the door, I heard the first gunshot go off.

"Shit!" Dyson yelled. Even though he'd been hit in his shoulder, he still managed to stay on his feet. He closed the door and locked it.

"Dyson! Are you okay?"

I stopped moving because I didn't want to leave him behind. Even though he was fighting through the pain, I could see the blood profusely soaking the sleeve of his t-shirt. He was losing too much blood way too fast.

"Just go, Mykah. Get to the garage. If I'm not down in a few seconds, take off, Go to your father's house and I'll meet you there," he instructed.

"My father's house? How do you even know where he stays?" I asked him.

He looked at me like I was dumb as hell to bring up the subject when two people were trying to kill us.

"Just go," he said as he threw his keys at me.

"No! I can't leave you like this, Dyson!"

"I'm used to this life, Mykah. And it'll only be a matter of seconds before they come in here so get the fuck out. Run! We'll meet up later."

He pushed me away from him with his good arm. Quickly, I ran towards the window with tears in my eyes. Bullets flew through the door at a rapid speed. I looked at Dyson one more time before climbing out of the window. I ran down the fire escape stairs and hit the alley towards the garage. The sounds of gunshots rang out like a fourth of July fireworks show.

Dyson only had one gun on him so I knew that the shots belonged to one of the masked men. Through a fit of tears, I hit the chirp on the key ring that Dyson gave me. It was his Ferrari, the fastest car in his fleet. I got in the car and started it immediately. I said a silent prayer for Dyson then sped away just as the men were running back out of his building.

Chapter 21

I cut Dyson's car off and sat in the driveway of Michael's house. When I left earlier, I had no clue that I would have to come back to this place so soon.

After avoiding it for years, it would now be my place of refuge until Dyson came to get me…that was if he survived the gunmen. I felt guilty for leaving him there to fight a battle that was meant for me.

I wiped the tears that fell down my face and pulled out my cell phone. I'd called him several times after pulling off but figured trying again made sense. I called him back to back but his voicemail kept picking up on the first ring.

Frustrated, I put the phone down and tried to think of a game plan just in case Dyson didn't make it. I needed to get myself together before I walked in the house. I pulled the visor mirror down and looked at my appearance. I looked like hell. I knew that Tayla and Michael would both have a lot of questions, but I wasn't in the mood to answer any of them. I really didn't want to talk to anybody. I just wanted to crawl up in a hole and die. It seemed like everything I loved seemed to leave me.

I got out of the car and looked around before walking towards the house. I had an eerie feeling that someone was watching me. I frantically knocked on the front door. I didn't know if anyone had followed me from Dyson's house and I didn't want to take the chance of someone running up on me. The last thing I needed right now was a surprise attack. After banging on the door for a minute or so, I tried to peek through the blinds of the living room but couldn't see much. The house was dark as hell. I guessed Tayla and Michael had gone out to eat, or were off to preach the good word. I still didn't get them as a couple but it was none of my business either way. My main concern was getting inside of the house so I could lay low until Dyson arrived. I walked around to the back to see if they'd locked the door, and to my surprise, it was still unlocked.

I walked in and grabbed the first towel I saw on the table. I needed to put some more ice on my nose and search the place for some sort of pain pills. After grabbing the ice tray and dumping all the ice on the towel, I placed it on my nose and walked to the living room. I hit each light switch I came across in the process. The house was too big and dark for me. It reeked of fresh cigar smoke, which I assumed was a habit of Michael's that he picked up when I left out of his life.

"Nice of you to join us," a deep voice suddenly boomed from the other side of the room.

I looked in the corner at the chair and was surprised to see none other than Preston LaRue. The smell of smoke came from the cigar that hung at the corner of his mouth. He was dressed in a three-piece suit that seemed specially tailored for his body. His right leg was crossed over his left one and his black crocodile square toe shoe shook at a steady pace. A gun sat on his lap and he was posted like he owned the damn place. It instantly felt like I was about to pass out. I sighed heavily and looked up at the ceiling waiting on a word from Michael's so called God. If the past few weeks hadn't already confirmed that God was not here for me, seeing Preston sitting there solidified it. I had no more fight left in me.

"Mr. LaRue, what umm, what are you doing here?" I asked nervously.

"Where's Dyson?" he returned.

"He's on his way. Did he tell you to meet me here, too? He probably thinks I can't handle myself and we'll need some help."

A little bit of hope filled my soul as I realized that Preston was actually here to help me. So maybe God was real or whatever.

"Help from what?" Preston roared as he sat up and put his cigar out.

The tone of his voice made my knees shake a little. He scared the hell out of me. I could see how it was so easy for him to run this city with little ease. I needed to remain calm so that he wouldn't kill me in a fit of rage.

"Umm…we were leaving and then we were ambushed. Dyson made me leave him, but he promised to meet me here. I'm sorry. I just assumed you knew and that's why you are here."

Preston glared at me while picking up his phone. I looked away because eye contact with him was too much.

"Dyson is in trouble. Get over to his South Side place and handle whatever the fuck he got going on. Call me back as soon as you know," he ordered into his phone.

Moments later, Preston disconnected the call and placed his attention back on me. He stared me up and down again as if his eyes were able to scan what kind of person I was. I felt uncomfortable under his scrutiny and wanted nothing more than for the moment to be over. My mind now raced again because he didn't seem like he knew what was going on with Dyson. If that was so, I had no idea why he would be at Michael's home, other than to handle some business with me. He seemed like a man who'd appreciate honesty so I began…

"If Dyson didn't send you for help, why are you here?"

"We were actually about to leave but then you showed up."

"We?"

He nodded. "I'm just glad to finally be in the presence of the woman who has my son on some weak shit."

"*We* were about to leave? Who is *we*?" I ignored the rest of his statement.

"You're direct and to the point. I like that. I guess your boldness is a trait that Dyson admired too," Preston added.

"I'm not interested in you trying to figure me out. Who the fuck is, we?" I asked again.

Preston tilted his head back and laughed. He reminded me of the first night I met Dyson and how he would do the same exact thing whenever I said something to him.

"I'm sure it's how feisty you are. Chauntelle was a bitch, but she lacked the feisty trait. It's always been a weakness for us LaRue men."

Preston was trying to dodge my question with his random talk. I stared him down with the intensity of a pit-bull. He chuckled again and clapped his hands in delight.

"She wants to know who we is, baby. Come on in." Preston turned towards the door.

My eyes followed his gaze. I waited to see who would come through the other side of the door. My mouth fell open when Michael stumbled out with a gun toting Tayla right behind him.

"Tayla, what the hell are you doing?" I asked with worry.

I looked at Michael realizing he was seconds from falling over. He had blood running down the front of his face as he held his side in pain.

"What do you think I'm doing, Mykah? I'm standing behind my man in loyalty. You know, that's some shit you aren't hip to," Tayla replied.

She pushed Michael further into the room but his fragile body couldn't handle the force. When he tumbled over on the floor, Tayla kicked him in anger.

"Calm down, pussy cat. What did I tell you about remaining in control," Preston said to her.

At that moment, Tayla walked towards him and placed a soft kiss on his lips. He wrapped his arms around her while keeping a close eye on me. I looked from him to Michael and was in disbelief of the situation. *So, Tayla was fucking with Preston LaRue?*

"Wait a minute. You and Preston are fucking around?" I asked.

They didn't have to confirm it verbally because her clinging under his arm with a wide grin on her face spoke all the words I needed to hear. My mind worked overtime trying to understand how and why? The shit had me lost and my expression showed my thoughts.

"Surprise!" Tayla said while laughing.

Michael groaned on the floor and tried to crawl his way towards the door. Tayla continued to laugh while walking up to him slowly. She pointed the gun at the back of his head and pulled the trigger before I even had time to blink.

"Oh my God, why the fuck did you do that?" I screamed, watching Michael's head hit the ground. A eerie feeling spread through my body, causing me to vomit. I hated Michael's guts, no lie, but there was no way that I wanted to see him die right in front of me. Not after everything he'd recently done for me. It was a long ass shot from being the father I needed, but I really was grateful that he attempted. I felt a lone tear fall down my face but quickly wiped it away. I never thought Michael's death would affect me, but somehow I was feeling a rush of some crazy emotions over it. I was pissed the fuck off that Tayla killed him in cold blood like that. He'd just declared his love for her.

"I know you're not crying," Tayla said while looking at me.

I didn't respond.

"He had to go. That was always the plan. I tried poisoning his ass, but that shit was taking too long. It was like watching paint dry. All of those damn hospital visits and doctor's appointments just to hear that the only progress I'd made was some vomiting, headaches and liver failure. Do you know how hard it is to get your hands onto some Troglitazone pills? That shit was frustrating," Tayla informed. "I gotta give it to him though, he's a tough old man."

I looked at Michael's lifeless body lying on the floor, then back at Tayla and Preston. I didn't understand what was going on. My mind couldn't even process what I just witnessed. This was just too much.

"What the hell is going on with you, Tayla? You were just saying how much you loved him and God, but now you love Preston?"

"Correction, I've always loved Preston. I didn't give a shit about Michael no more than you did. Everything I did over these past few months was for Preston and Preston only!" she yelled at me.

I shook my head in disbelief. Tayla encouraged me to kill Dyson but she was in love with his father. That shit made no sense. The Tayla that stood in front of me was someone that I did not know. The look in her eyes told me that she enjoyed killing Michael. I remembered the feeling that I had when I killed my first man. It was a euphoric moment, almost as if invisible chains had been broken and I was now free to do as I pleased. Now Tayla was wrapped in it. I knew from experience, once the adrenaline slowed down, she would feel like shit. That was the downside to being a killer.

Even though my mind was all over the place I couldn't help but notice how well put together Tayla looked. The diamond studs in her ears were huge. She'd dropped a few pounds and was draped from head to toe in Chanel. Her style instantly reminded me of Chauntelle. She'd definitely been upgraded.

"You have no idea what you just did, Tayla. I hope you really do know God because you for damn sure are going to need him to help you get over this," I said sympathetically.

She laughed again while Preston stared back and forth at the both of us like he was disgusted. I didn't know if I should focus more on Tayla's unstable ass or Preston's creepy ass. Either way, I also knew there was a good possibility that I wouldn't make it out alive. I couldn't see Preston leaving me as a witness. He never left witnesses. But I needed answers before they killed me though. I couldn't die without knowing why Tayla had decided to marry then kill Michael.

"Mykah, to be as smart as you are, you are so clueless. I've been planning Michael's death since day one. You think it was easy for me to pretend to be in love with his old ass? Preston is the only reason I was able to do it. Michael had something that Preston needed, but Michael wouldn't budge. This is all his fault. If he would've just given up the church, we wouldn't be here," she replied. "He was so damn stubborn."

"You did all this shit for his church? You killed him because of that?"

"How the fuck can you judge me, Mykah? You killed men for Lady and I killed a man for Preston. The only difference is I'm getting dicked down in the process and getting major cash daily," Tayla stated like it was no big deal.

"Wow, you're more fucked up than I thought, Tayla. Now that Michael is dead, genius how do you plan on getting any of the church's money?"

"We only needed the church to clean up some money," she spat. "We don't need Michael's little ass coins. But since Michael didn't want to give it up he had to go. Thankfully, I had him sign over everything to me in case of his untimely demise. Besides, they had an old beef that runs deep, something you'll never understand."

"An old beef? Wait, this is too much." I looked over at Preston for answers.

"Let's just say, Michael disrespected me for years and me allowing him to live this long was a gift. It was time for him to go," he added harshly.

"Unlike you, I got the job done," Tayla interjected. "I killed my target but look at you. You standing here love sick over Dyson when you were supposed to kill him," Tayla announced.

Preston cleared his throat and a thick vein pulsated from the side of his neck. Hearing that I was supposed to kill Dyson set off a new flare of rage in him.

"Shut the fuck up Tayla and go and get your bags. You've said more than enough," Preston ordered.

Tayla cut the laughter and quickly sprung into action. It was clear Preston had power over her just like everyone else. She obeyed his command with no back talk. I took a few steps backwards. I wanted to make a dash for the door, but knew Preston would shoot me before I even cleared it.

"So, someone hired you to kill Dyson, huh?" At that point, Preston walked over to the window and looked outside. "Where is he? It's strange how you show up here in his car but he's nowhere to be found. Give me a good reason to not shoot your lying ass. Where the fuck is my son?"

"He's on his way, I promise. I know you heard Tayla say that I was supposed to kill him, but it was something that I just couldn't do because I fell in love with him."

"Save it! You two barely know each other. You're in love with his dick. LaRue men have been known to put a pounding down.

"I promise he isn't dead," I uttered frightfully. "He told me he would be here and I believe him. Just give him some time." I prayed my assumptions were true.

"It really is a damn shame that I have to kill you. I've been watching you over the years. Lady did a pretty good job with you. You're smart and sexy as hell, a deadly combination. I could use a woman like you on my team but unfortunately for you, your reign ends tonight," Preston replied.

When he pointed his gun at me, I immediately began to beg for my life.

"Listen, I don't know what I walked in on and don't care. This has nothing to do with me. Just let me go."

"Actually, it has everything to do with you. I would be a fool to leave a woman with your talents alive. There would be nothing to stop you from trying to kill me."

"I wouldn't do that. I'm in love with Dyson. I know he has a great deal of respect for you and he would never forgive me if I did that!" I yelled out.

"Yeah, but I can't take that chance. The only reason you're still alive is because I thought Dyson was trying to recruit you. Had I known that you were trying to kill him, you would have been dead a long time ago. It wasn't personal at first, just business but Dyson always makes it personal."

For what seemed like the millionth time that day, I was staring down the barrel of a gun. I knew I couldn't keep cheating death so I embraced the inevitable. Fuck it! I hear so many people scream how you only live once and my only regret was the way I treated Jamison and my girls. Other than that, I had a good life and I wasn't about to further beg for it. Preston and Tayla would not get that satisfaction out of me. I held my head up and stared Preston directly in the eyes.

"Go ahead, handle your fucking business," I finally said.

Preston smiled and nodded his head at me like he was proud. I had his respect and since we both knew the game, I knew that didn't change a thing. I braced myself for death when suddenly the door flew open. Both Preston and me were startled as we stared in that direction. When I saw Dyson walk through the threshold I almost fainted. His shirt was covered in blood and he could barely stand up without having to use the door for support.

"Pops, I wouldn't do that if I were you. Put the gun down."

Chapter 22

I'd never been so happy to see a man in all my life. Seeing him reassured me that I was going to be okay and he would be able to help get me out of town. I quickly went to Dyson and helped him walk into the house. I sat him down in the chair and pulled the bloody shirt off of him. I looked over his shoulder and saw where the bullet entered his body. I pushed him up slightly to see if there was an exit wound as well. When I saw it, I turned to Preston and gave him a weak smile. He still had his gun pointed at me but his eyes were focused on Dyson.

"What the fuck happened to you?" Preston asked his son.

"Muthafuckas tried to hem me up. Ain't shit I couldn't handle though," he replied.

"What muthafuckas? You don't have any beef that I don't know about," Preston questioned.

Dyson closed his eyes and avoided the question. He obviously didn't want to tell Preston that the beef was mine. When we were at his apartment he kept insisting that we had to get out of there as soon as possible. He also told me there was a bounty placed on my head but he never said by whom, so the guys had to be there for me.

"He's lost a lot of blood but the bullet went in and straight out. I need some peroxide and something to stop this bleeding," I said frantically.

"Tayla, bring a first aid kit and some towels in here now!" Preston yelled angrily.

He sat the gun down on the table and paced the floor back and forth. I could see that someone trying to kill Dyson had pissed him off. The streets of St. Louis would bleed tonight until the responsible party was dealt with.

"Dyson, baby. I'm so glad you made it. I was so scared. Why the fuck did you make me leave? I could have helped you."

He grabbed my hand and kissed it. We stared at each other for a few seconds until he closed his eyes and held his shoulder.

"Mykah, we gotta go. I gotta get you out of here," he said between short breaths.

"You're not going anywhere but to Dr. Stevens. He can patch you up in his house. We have some business to handle," Preston said while picking up his phone and walking into the hallway.

Tayla came back into the living room with several bags and the items that I needed for Dyson. She gave them to me and tried to assist me. I pushed her hands away. I didn't need her fucking help. I now hated her. I thought about her involvement with my husband and kids, wondering what else she'd done.

"I'm just trying to help, Mykah. If he dies, you do realize that your life won't be spared. Preston is furious," she whispered in my ear.

"I don't give a fuck about him. Dyson is my only concern right now."

I brushed her off my shoulder and continued to work on Dyson. He'd lost a lot of blood, so I tied a piece of the towel around his arm firmly. If he had any chance of staying alive, stopping his blood flow was his only option.

"Dyson, get up! You're leaving now. I have a car on the way for you," Preston commanded.

"I'm not leaving Mykah," Dyson replied.

"This bitch is disposable. You can find one with a lot less baggage so get your ass up and get ready to go!" Preston yelled again.

"I'm not leaving her! I promised I would get her out of this shit. My word is everything, ain't that what you say, Pops!" Dyson yelled back at him.

I could tell he was still in a great deal of pain and watching him talk shit to Preston on my behalf made me feel good on the inside. Tayla just stood next to Preston looking like a deaf mute. She didn't speak or listen unless Preston told her what to do.

"Don't be a fucking idiot Dyson. You have always been weak as fuck when it comes to a woman. I did nothing when you married that good for nothing ass Chauntelle but I'm not about to let you throw your life away for this bitch. You don't even know her."

Dyson stood up in front of me. He was chest to chest with Preston. He wanted him to know that he was protecting me at all cost.

"How the fuck are you gone tell me who I know? I'm just as much a man as you. So what I don't beat on women, or walk around yelling around shit for other people to do. This is my woman and I'm standing by her."

"See that's the problem. You don't stand by a woman but in front of her. I always knew you would be the weakest link. It's the pitiful way you came into this world, lost and without a mother. As a man, you have to know how to handle your fucking business," Preston stated.

Dyson had a perplexed look spread across his face. But before he could respond, Preston turned his gun on Tayla and shot her at point blank range in the head. Her body fell to the floor and Preston never even blinked. It was the true definition of an assassination.

"Oh my God!" I yelled out in shock.

Seeing Michael die was bad but watching my former best friend hit the floor almost killed me too. I was mad as hell at Tayla and probably would've never spoken a single word to her again, but I didn't want her to die. I was hysterical and cried uncontrollably. I wanted to look away from her but my eyes couldn't tear away from the vision of her bloody face on the floor.

"Now, that's how you handle your fucking business with a woman. They don't mean shit. The quicker you learn that, the more successful you'll be," Preston boasted.

He wasn't the least bit fazed about killing Tayla. I guess some would call it poetic justice for how she killed Michael with no regard. Tayla obviously thought Preston loved her, but it seemed as if he was only in it for money. With Tayla now dead, he would just step in and take the church. He clearly didn't need nor love her.

"Pops, I swear, if you lay one hand on her I will never fuck with you again."

"Bitches are always last on the food chain. Loyalty and money, Dyson. Didn't I teach you any fucking thing?"

"You right Pops, I'm clearly not thinking straight," Dyson said before turning to me. "I'm sorry Mykah but I can't put you before my family."

I continued to cry as I realized that Dyson was going to kill me. I loved him, lost my family because of him and now he was going to kill me. Had I not been so hurt I would have laughed at the irony of one of my targets actually killing me. I'd been a fool in so called lust.

Suddenly, Dyson raised his gun and pointed it at me. Preston smiled and stood behind him before coaxing him on proudly.

"That's my boy. Kill this bitch so we can get you out of here and patched up. You'll find some new trim in no time."

I wouldn't close my eyes this time though. I wanted my eyes to be something that he remembered. We stared at each other for a few seconds before he lifted the gun in the air and then winked at me. At that point, he turned around and came down on Preston's head with it. Preston folded like paper in the wind. As soon as he hit the ground, Dyson pulled me into his good arm and hugged me tightly.

"His men are on the way so we have to go like right now. We gonna take my Cutlass because that damn Ferarri is too flashy," he informed.

"Let's go. There's just something I have to do first."

Chapter 23

"This shit is crazy, Mykah. I'm telling you that we have to leave St. Louis as soon as possible. You on some crazy shit right now. I don't know how I let you talk me into this shit!" Dyson fussed. "What if the police are in there, or one of them niggas who tried to ambush us? I only popped one, but I only hit his leg so you working with two sets of evil here. Them or the police!" Dyson yelled at me.

"You're being overly paranoid, baby. How would those men even know to look for me at the hospital? Speaking of that, how the hell did you get out of there alive?"

"Because whoever they were couldn't shoot worth shit. Once I popped the smaller one, the other fool took off running barely grabbing the injured nigga. These new school muthafuckas don't know the first thing about putting in serious work."

"I guess we should thank the universe for that. I was so afraid that you weren't going to show up."

"I always keep my word, baby. Why the fuck you think I'm on this sucka shit taking you to see your ex while I'm hurt and still bleeding?"

He tried unsuccessfully for the past few minutes to talk me out of going to see Jamison at the hospital, but I couldn't leave without apologizing to him. Dyson was just frustrated that he was sticking his neck out for me and I seemed to be still hung up on Jamison. Nothing could have been further than the truth. I was ready to leave everything behind me and ride it out with Dyson, but my conscious wouldn't let me go without me being able to clear my heart with Jamison. I wanted him to know Malia had taken the money, but they could have it.

"It's not what you think, Dyson. I need to do this. He didn't deserve what I did to him. He never did anything wrong to me. I can see that now and I want him to know that I realize it."

Dyson looked at me in the rearview mirror and shook his head at me as he turned into the parking lot of the hospital. We'd stopped at a Family Dollar store on the way where I picked up a pair of scrubs and some scissors. As he drove like a madman down the highway, I put the uniform on and tried my hardest to cut my shoulder length hair in a bob with the dull scissors. I didn't know if the thousands of people who were at the hospital saw my picture so I wanted to look different.

"You know the police be all over this place so I'm letting you out and I'll be over in Forest Park. You have fifteen minutes and that's it. I gotta get patched up. Besides, Preston won't stay knocked out for long. We need to be long gone when he wakes up," Dyson said.

"Okay, damn. I promise I won't be long."

I hopped out of the car and gave him a smile. Since stopping the blood from flowing from his shoulder wound, Dyson seemed to be doing a little better, but sweat still dripped down from his head. He needed some rest. I walked across the lot and into the hospital.

I knew that Jamison was probably on the black out floor because he was the victim of a crime. There was no way to get on that floor without swiping a badge. The hospital was chaotic with visiting hours ending soon. I looked at the main corridor where the elevators were noticing plenty of doctors and nurses hanging around in the halls. I walked towards them and pretended to be waiting on the elevators as well. A group of chatty nurses stood next to me gossiping about their co-workers. I pretended to stumble and bump into them. We all shifted forward and I used the opportunity to snatch the ID of the young black girl who was doing the most talking.

"Oh no. Excuse me, I'm so embarrassed," I said to them sheepishly.

"You're good. No problem at all," she responded.

The elevator came and they all immediately rushed into it. I backed away from the elevators and made my way towards the stairs.

"Excuse me, Miss!" one of them yelled to my back.

I walked faster trying to get out of their eyesight but she was persistent.

"Ma'am. Excuse me. Can someone stop that woman in the green scrubs?" she continued to yell across the hall.

I clipped the badge to the bottom of the inside of my shirt and spun around to face them. If they were going to accuse me of swiping the badge, I didn't want to make it easy for them by confessing.

"Yes?" I asked.

"I was just trying to tell you that the tag is still on your shirt. Have a good day," she said before waving and letting the elevator button go.

I wanted to chase her down and slap the hell out of her for scaring me like that. Instead, I spun around angrily and walked over to the stairwell. I hit the four flights in record time. Dyson said I only had fifteen minutes and I'd already wasted five of those trying to figure out how to get access to Jamison's floor. I swiped the badge and was disappointed when the light didn't change green on the door. I took my time and swiped again. This time the light blinked green.

I walked on the floor and looked around realizing that I didn't even know what room Jamison was in. I turned towards my right, walking past each room looking for him. I couldn't tell who was who because everyone for the most part was hooked up to all kinds of tubes and machines. I looked around for the patient's board that the doctor's used and was happy to see that J. Rice was the first one on there.

I walked towards his room and peeked in the door way making sure no one was in there with him. Seeing Jamison lying in the bed, breathing with the help of a ventilator almost knocked me on my ass. His face was slightly swollen and there were numerous cuts on his body. His left arm was in a cast and suspended in the air. I walked to the side of his bed and grabbed his hand. I stood in shock, unable to believe that I'd done that to him. I didn't even have to talk to the doctors to know that he was barely alive.

"Jamison, I'm so sorry. I can't believe I did this. I wish you could hear me. I really did love you and I didn't mean for any of this to happen," I cried.

I paused and waited as if he would miraculously wake up and say that he forgave me.

"I have to go but I'll be back. I'm sure Lucille and Malia are going to take good care of you. I'm so sorry, baby. I love you."

I kissed his hand softly and stood up. I had to get out of there and fast. I was already at the fifteen-minute mark and I knew Dyson would not wait forever.

I walked out of the room and was headed back to the stairwell when suddenly I heard a loud beeping noise go off. It only took seconds for several nurses and a doctor rush past me. I turned around and saw them flying into Jamison's room. I stood paralyzed as I heard them try to revive him several times. T

ears filled my eyes again and I tried to blink them away. I turned around quickly and was shocked when I saw Lucille running down the hallway as well. She ran straight past me not realizing who I was. I almost didn't know who she was either because for the first time, she looked sober and somewhat healthy.

She ran into Jamison's room, but a nurse quickly ushered her back into the hallway. She was crying loudly and each shrill did something to me. I felt guilty as hell. I wondered where Malia was because Lucille needed support from someone. Knowing that she was dealing with this Jamison situation all alone made me feel worse.

I opened the door to the stairwell but was stopped by Lucille's hysterical shrieks. My heart told me that Jamison had died and they were unable to bring him back. I said a prayer for Jamison and quickly flew down the steps and out of the hospital. I ran so fast that my tears felt like rain drops flying off my skin. I didn't stop running until I made it to the spot where Dyson said he would be parked.

There was no car and no Dyson. It was only me and the trees of the park. I looked around to see if I was in the wrong area, but the park was completely empty. My heart sank as I concluded that Dyson had left me. The only lil bit of money I had left was in that car. I had nothing and nowhere to go. I sat on the bench and accepted my fate. I would be dead by the morning. Someone had a bounty on my head and now Preston LaRue's men had probably found Dyson and were looking for me as well.

Now what the fuck am I supposed to do?

I didn't have long to ponder on the thought when suddenly a silver Mercedes CL swooped in front of me and two men hopped out.

Normally, I would have fought with all of my might but with the kind of day I had, I wasn't going to prolong the inevitable. I didn't even attempt a swing as one of them grabbed me roughly while the other placed a bag over my head. They tied my hands behind my back and threw me into the back of the trunk. I closed my eyes and prayed to Michael's God.

Chapter 24

"Well, where is she? You didn't kill her did you?"

"Man, chill the fuck out. She's in the other room. I didn't lay a hand on that bitch," a male voice sounded.

"That's the same thing you said about Dyson and now he's bleeding all over the fucking place."

"Well, how else were we supposed to get him in the car? Did you think that nigga was gonna get in on his own? Malia, just give me my money so we can burn the fuck out. I don't know what the fuck you on and it ain't my concern, but that nigga about to die and them crazy ass LaRues gone be all over the place. I'm bout to lay low."

"Yeah okay, lay low my ass. You betta answer the phone if I need you to dispose of the bodies."

"Don't I always answer the phone? Didn't I answer the phone when you called and asked to use my car so you could run that bitch over?"

"Look, Ray, don't act like you didn't get paid for that. I even paid you to follow her around."

"Well, I didn't sign up for no LaRue drama, so leave me outta that shit. What kinda person goes after their own family?" the male voice asked.

I strained to hear the voices outside of the door. With the wall between us muffling the sound, I couldn't hear their exact words but knew my daughter's voice. Shock sped through my body confusing every thought I possibly came up with.

"Mykah, Mykah you need to get up," a voice said weakly from another part of the room.

I couldn't see who it was because the bag was still over my face, but I knew the voice belonged to Dyson. He sounded like he was in a great deal of pain.

"Oh my God Dyson. Are you okay?"

"Yeah, I'm good for the most part."

"Where are we?"

"I don't know. Awww shit," he said in pain.

"Do you know how many people are out there?" I whispered back to him.

"Two dudes and a girl. We gotta get the fuck out of here," he managed to say.

My mind raced trying to figure out what I could do. I didn't have the heart to tell him I heard my daughter's voice in that other room. My hands were still tied behind me as I wiggled my wrists trying to free myself from the rope. Whichever one of them tied me up, needed to find another profession. It was loosely done and the rope fell off with little effort. I sat up and removed the bag that covered my face.

I looked around in the room trying to adjust my eyes to the dim light. There was nothing in the room that could give me any clues as to where I was. Dyson was lying on the floor in a puddle of his own blood. His face was badly bruised. There was so much blood coming from his head that I couldn't see the color of his hair. After losing as much as he did earlier, he would more than likely pass out soon. I didn't want to scare him by my reaction, but he looked close to death. I crawled over to him and placed his head in my lap. I couldn't stop myself from crying. This situation was bad...really bad.

"I'm going to fix this. I swear I am. Just hold on," I said to him while kissing his cheek.

All of a sudden, the door swung open and my mouth flew open. To say I was in shock was an understatement. I blinked my eyes several times as if that would change the scene in front of me.

"Hello, Mother," Malia said to me with her hands on her hips.

I stared at her with no words to speak as she glared back at me with a wicked look. She looked good. She was dressed in an all black jumpsuit that hugged her body like a glove, and her neck and ears were draped with diamonds. She had her hair pulled back into a ponytail, and her face was full of professional applied makeup. She looked like the perfect replica of me.

"I get that you may not want to talk to me. I totally understand that but you owe me a conversation where you actually pay attention," she said, limping into the room.

"What the hell are you doing, Malia? Why are we here?" I asked her.

It was the only thing I could think to say as I stared at the gun on her side and one in her hand. What she was doing was apparent. Why she was doing it was another question.

"This is the only way I could get your attention. You're so fucking self absorbed that you forgot about not only your husband but your kids as well."

"So, you stole my money and kidnapped me so you can talk? Couldn't you just call me?"

She threw her head back and laughed at me. I didn't see what was so funny, but I let her have her moment.

"So, you know about the money thing, huh? That was a brilliant idea if I do say so myself but this ain't about that right now. This is about what a bitch you were to us and how you ruined our fucking lives. That's what this is about!" she yelled.

"Malia, I'm sorry. I really am, but he needs medical attention. He's about to die," I pleaded with her.

"I don't give a damn if he dies. I proved that earlier when I shot him in the shoulder. He's lucky he got one off and hit me in my leg. That's the only reason he's here now, bleeding out a slow death. I figure that will torture you a little more to see your latest boy-toy die in front of you."

My eyes enlarged. "So, wait a minute. You were the one who came to Dyson's house? But I don't understand. How do you even know how to shoot a gun? Where the fuck did you get it from? How do you know the men who kidnapped me? That same car tried to kill me twice." I asked her all of the questions that danced around in my head.

There were so many of them and I wanted answers to every last one. I waited as she just smirked at me.

"I was the one who tried to hit you with that car, of course with help. Lady arranged it all, and my boy Ray helped us pull it off. But I must say, you really are quick on your feet. As far as how I know how to shoot a gun, well Lady taught me. Apparently being a cold heartless killer runs in the family."

"Malia, what are you talking about? And why are you doing this?"

"The question is, why not? You deserve everything that's happened to you. Karma is a bitch and unfortunately for you that bitch is your daughter. And by the way, I was the one who had your car stolen, and spray painted whore on the ground."

I sat with my mouth wide open as she confessed.

Dyson let out a low groan of pain. His body shook wildly on the floor. He was going into shock. I tried to turn to him but Malia stopped me.

"Didn't I say don't fucking move!" she screamed.

"I need to get Dyson some help."

"You need to get Dyson some help? Really? You fucking smashed into our car and killed my sister. Plus, you left the scene without looking back but you want me to save this nigga's life!" Malia yelled angrily.

"What do you mean killed your sister? Tayla said you died not Jasmine. Where is she?" I asked her frantically.

"She's at the fucking funeral home, that's where dead people go, Mother."

I felt my heart slow its beating pattern. The pain in the pit of my stomach was unbearable. My sweet baby Jasmine. There was no way I could have killed her. I looked at Malia with tears running down my face. I wanted her to tell me that she was just saying that to fuck with me but when I saw her own tears start to form, I knew this was very real. My heart ached with an agonizing sting.

"Oh my God. I didn't know. They said you died. I could handle you dying but not Jasmine. "Noooooooooo, pleaseeeee nooooooooo," I hollered. My baby never did anything to anyone. Please Lord, not my sweet baby," I mumbled through my tears.

"You are so fucking pathetic, I swear. What kind of parent says shit like that? I always felt like you didn't like me but I could never understand why. Now I know it's because you're jealous of me. Daddy loved me and so did Jasmine. You'd do anything to take that from me," Malia said while wiping her eyes.

I ignored her as I cried for the loss of my child. She was the only person who loved me unconditionally. I would never forgive myself for killing her. Death was all around me. It seemed to mock me for all the senseless killings I had committed. Dyson grunted on the floor again. His moans of pain snapped me out of my trance and I looked at him sadly. I didn't want to see anyone else die.

"Malia, we need to call for him some help right now," I continued to cry not only for him but for the loss of Jasmine. That was something I would never be able to get over.

"I don't give a shit if he dies within the next few seconds. It's not my fucking problem it's yours. I'm hoping I can send you to Hell before he gets there."

She shrugged her shoulders and tightened her grip on the gun. The arrogant smirk on her face made me want to take my chances and lunge at her but she seemed way too unstable. Talking sense into her seemed like the only reasonable thing to do.

"Malia, baby please calm down. It's just that Dyson is from a very powerful family and if he dies, someone will have to pay for this. Just let me call for help," I pleaded.

"I swear if you make another move, I'm going to blow your ass to pieces," she said through clenched teeth.

"I'm so sorry Malia. I won't move just please put the gun down. We can work this out."

"Did you know I used to cry myself to sleep every single night because my mother wasn't home? You never showed any interest in us. No dance recitals, parent conferences…nothing. You weren't even there when my period came on. Do you know how embarrassing it is for a girl to have her father show her how to wear a fucking pad? Do you? I used to wonder where the fuck you were. Why didn't you care? Why I couldn't have a normal mother instead of the cock sucking whore I was born to?"

Her comments stung like hell. It felt like she had pushed a wrecking ball inside of my soul as tears poured down her face causing her mascara and eyeliner to make a dark trail down the sides of her cheeks.

My daughter was in so much pain. I was too as I thought about her comments and what I'd done to Jasmine.

"Maila, I loved you the best way I knew how. I didn't have a mother. I was left stuck with a father who didn't want nor love me. I didn't even know what love was until Jamison gave it to me, and even then I didn't know how to give it back." By now, we were both sobbing like newborn babies.

"This is not about you! What part of that don't you understand? When you decided to have kids you gave up that right to feel sorry for yourself. I gave you warnings and chances to get your shit right. Those text messages you got came from me. I was thinking maybe you would be scared enough to leave all that other shit alone and just be with your damn family but no, you don't have a heart."

"I swear I wish I could do it all over again. I didn't mean to kill Jasmine nor Jamison. You have to forgive me. You're all I have left," I said softly.

Malia's confessions had stabbed me repeatedly in my heart. I'd really failed my kids the same way that my parents failed me. My mother would still be alive if she'd loved me more than Michael. I had somehow repeated the same fucked up cycle that I vowed never to do.

"Wait, Daddy ain't dead. Yeah, he's in a coma but he ain't dead. I was just at the hospital with him last night," Malia replied angrily.

I realized that Lucille hadn't told her that Jamison was dead. I tried to look away from her, but she caught the expression on my face. Her eyes welled up with tears once again.

"No, no. You're lying. I swear you'll say any fucking thing to hurt someone!"

Malia began to take short breaths as if she couldn't catch her breath.

"I'm so sorry baby. I didn't mean for any of this to happen."

Malia ignored my remark while she continued to struggle to breathe. She closed her eyes and took in the loss of Jamison. She was finally unraveling. If I was going to make a move to escape, it would have to be now. I felt a tug at my heart because I knew this was a low down option for me, but I just couldn't see myself dying this way.

Suddenly, I rushed her causing both of us to fall to the floor. The gun went off scaring her. Malia jumped from the sound as I wrestled the gun from her hand. I didn't want to point the gun at her, but she was fighting me so hard that I had no other choice. Even though she'd assisted with making my life a living hell recently, I couldn't shoot her like I would anyone else. She tried unsuccessfully to throw me off of her but I wouldn't move.

"Calm down, Malia. I don't want to hurt you but if you make me, I will. I understand you hate me, but you need to fall the fuck back into the place of a child. You got the money, just take it and go on and live your life. I don't want it," I said to her.

After a few more attempts to push me away, she finally stopped fighting me. She sat there for a few seconds. However, just when I thought she'd calmed down, Malia spat directly in my face. When I slapped the shit out of her, the look of shock on her face showed me that she really hated me.

"You better kill me now because when I make it out of here my mission will be to kill you on site," she growled.

I looked in her eyes and was scared to see the same look that I had when I first started. I was so angry and eager to kill whoever to make myself feel better. It was kind of scary to look at but I believed her when she said that she would kill me. She hated me just as I hated Michael.

"I hate you feel that way. I also hate what I'm gonna have to do next but you leave me no choice."

"Do it. I don't give a damn. You may as well kill me just like you did Daddy and Jasmine. You gone get what's coming to you because I'm the least of your problems," Malia responded.

I raised the gun, aimed it directly at her heart, then said a prayer for God to forgive me. I never really wanted his approval, but I now realized that only He would be able to help me.

"I love you and I'm sorry," I said one last time.

"Get the fuck off that girl now!" a voice yelled out in the doorway.

When I turned around, I stared in total shock. I had to be seeing things because this wasn't right. I shook my head thinking that would clear out the hallucination but she was still there.

"Lady?"

Chapter 25

"The one and fuckin' only. Now get the fuck off that girl and back up," she said to me while walking in the room.

I looked at the gun she pointed at me. I couldn't understand what was going on. I had never been more confused in all my life. *Lady was dead*, I thought. She burned in the fire. They had a memorial service for her. That much I knew was true.

"But you're dead," I said still in a state of confusion.

"How many times I done told you every closed eye ain't sleep? Death don't look this damn good," she replied.

I scanned her from head to toe. She looked damn good. She had on a pair of black wide leg gauchos, a black lace shirt and a tailored black blazer. Her eyes were hidden behind a pair of Versace mirrored shades. She leaned on her black cane that was covered in diamonds. She even ditched her normal blonde wig for a short, spiked red one. She looked like new money.

"I don't get this. Why'd you fake your death and where you been?"

"Mykah, it's like you never listened to a damn thing I said. There is always a bigger picture. No matter how small shit seems, it always adds up to some major shit. It's been right in your face the entire time."

She shook her head at me and gave me her infamous look that proved she was disappointed with me. She wanted me to draw my own conclusions.

"None of this makes sense. I was there at the building when the fire broke out. They said you didn't get out."

"I had my grandson knock out that crack-head whore of his for a little package and she the one who went up in smoke. But what difference it make to you? Yo' ass didn't even show up for the services. Them damn fools put on a nice production for me. Course I had to watch it from afar, but from what I saw that shit was mighty fancy," she said with a smile on her face.

"I still don't get why you did this though."

Forgetting that I was on top of Malia, I loosened my grip on her. Of course her rowdy ass used that to her advantage. She made a move and before I realized what happened, I had fallen off of her. She immediately went for the gun. She grabbed it and stood up laughing like a madwoman.

"This shit just got real interesting. I need some popcorn. I told you, your ass shoulda killed me when you had the chance," Malia stated while shrugging her shoulders.

"Watch yo' damn mouth, girl, and go and get me a chair. My gout flarin' up from all this damn stress y'all puttin' me in," Lady said to her.

Malia quickly walked out of the room. Lady hobbled over to Dyson and shook her head at him. I didn't move as I watched her poke him in the side with her cane. He moved his body slightly and even though I was happy to see he was barely hanging on, I couldn't focus on that because I was still in shock from seeing Lady alive.

"You done got yourself in a real bad way there, Dyson. I hate to see you laying up like this, son, but this had to happen. Everybody has an expiration date."

Dyson opened his eyes and stared at Lady. He was too weak to talk but I could read the many questions in his eyes. He was just as shocked as I was to see Lady.

"You're a hard guy to kill," she blurted, then quickly turned her attention back on me.

So many questions filled my head. But Lady had gotten up close in my face.

"Mykah, I been watchin' you carry on asshole backwards these past few weeks. You been sloppier than prostituted pussy. I'm ashamed to even attach your name to mine in the condition you in. I bred you to be the best in this shit and what the fuck you do, throw it all away on the idea of some bullshit called love. Now you see why I been so against that shit. Look what it got you. Look what the hell it got my son. Hell, look what the fuck it got me."

Malia came back in with the chair and took it to Lady. Lady sat down and quickly took off the black loafers that were on her feet. Malia stood behind her with a smirk on her face. I could see that they were apparently a team but what I didn't understand was Lady's motive.

"What son? What in the hell are you talking about, Lady?" I questioned.

"Initially, I was just gone disappear without saying shit to nobody but I'm tired of sticking my neck out just to get hung. You just like yo damn daddy, Mykah. No fucking loyalty in you at all. I gave you the better half of my life. I didn't have to look out for you but I did that shit anyway. I was that bitch when your weak ass Mama couldn't handle playing second fiddle to me. She owed me that shit. They took my baby from me and I was gone do everything in my power to make their ass pay for it."

"Who took your baby? And when?"

She sat back in the chair and crossed her arms with a cocky smile on her face, ignoring my questions. I didn't know this Lady. The woman who sat before me was nothing more than a stranger. I couldn't figure out what angle to take with her.

"Lady, I don't know what's going on here. First Malia has lost her mind and now you talking about all this shit that I apparently have nothing to do with. I just want to get Dyson some help, that's all. You can do whatever you want to me after that but please get him some help before he dies," I cried.

"Oh, you are very much involved in this. You been there since the night the shit all went down. Yo Mama and me, we were so damn happy to be pregnant at the same time. She and Michael had been living together for about 6 months when we both found out. Michael was mine first, but yo mama did everything in her power to take him away from me, but he never left me all the way. We were in love and I wanted Michael so bad that I allowed him to play house over there with her, and sleep with me when her pussy dried up.

"The night we both went into labor and had them babies she was devastated to see Michael standing by my side as my son came out first. He held him in his arms and the look of pride that filled that man swelled my heart up. It was like yo mama saw our love for each other for the first time. She pitched such a fit she passed out soon as she had you. I didn't care though because all I knew was my baby boy was the most beautiful thing I ever did see. I remember holding his lil fingers as he drifted off to sleep. He had a birthmark on his right arm that was shaped like the state of Texas. I remember staring at it 'foe I drifted off to sleep. I wake up a few hours later and he gone. Michael told me he passed away in his sleep."

I stared at Lady with wide, wild eyes. Dyson had the same birthmark that she described on his arm. My stomach churned and I immediately spit up what little food I had in my stomach. I had slept with and fallen in love with my own fucking brother. I wiped my mouth with the back of my hand and shook my head in disbelief.

"Lady, please tell me that Dyson is not your son. Please tell me he is not my brother. Oh my God. What the fuck did you guys do to our lives? He can't be Michael's son, he's a fucking Larue," I cried.

I felt so sick to my stomach that I thought I would pass out. Lady just continued to smile at me as if my misery over this story was some kind of gratification for her.

"How fucking evil and demented would that be if I let that shit go on? I know I've done some sick shit in my life but damn give me some credit. Dyson is definitely a LaRue. When Michael was spending his time playing husband of the year, I was being kept by Preston. Michael had no clue though and from what I found out, Preston barged in that house when he heard I gave birth and bitch slapped Michael around. He threatened his punk ass and Michael let that son of a bitch walk out the house with my baby that he took home to his barren ass wife to raise."

I was somewhat relieved to hear that Preston was definitely Dyson's father but the story still didn't make sense. It still didn't add up to why Lady would fake her death and why she was determined to let her own son die on the floor at her feet.

"Lady, we have a lot of unanswered questions here but I can't focus on any of that until I get Dyson some help first," I said again.

"That's not going to happen, Mykah. I need for Dyson to die so Preston can feel the pain I felt to have a baby ripped from my arms. I don't have any attachment to Dyson. I didn't even know he was my son until a few months ago. That's when I came up with a plan for revenge on not only Preston but Michael's ass as well. He was supposed to love and protect me. He let that man walk in there and snatch my baby and didn't even have the decency to tell me what really happened. Yet he continued to lay up with me for years. If anybody is demented and evil, it's Michael and Preston and for that, their children will pay for their sins."

She raised her gun at me and I panicked slightly. There were still so many unanswered questions and I needed to know the answers.

"You were the one who stole my money, weren't you?" I asked her.

"That was actually me," Malia butted in. "Never forget that, Mother Dear. But it was Lady's idea. When she brought it up, I agreed immediately. I knew nothing would hurt you fucking more than not having that money you worship so damn much," she spat maliciously.

"One more slip of that damn tongue and I'm cuttin' it out. You may disrespect yo' damn mammy, but that shit won't fly this way lil' birdy," Lady reprimanded her.

Malia shrunk down and lowered her head. Lady was like her grandmother so she knew that her threats were serious.

"Lady, why would you do this to me?"

"Finding out Dyson was really my son, done something to me. I guess I caught a case of revenge. I got the brilliant idea to send Chauntelle to you when she came sniffin' around my way about a way to get away from Dyson. I knew you would take on that assignment and I was hopin' you would off him, so I could slip the info to the LaRues and they would kill you. I was gone sit back and laugh at how much pain this incident would cause and the best part would be the new beef it would start between Preston and Michael."

"I can't believe this shit," I mumbled to myself.

All of the pieces of how chaotic my life became fell together in my mind. I now understood the bigger picture that Lady was talking about. I wished I could go back to that day Chauntelle showed up to my office. I would toss her out on her ass.

"You better believe it, baby! Michael got real greedy and decided to blackmail Preston about what happened the night he stole Dyson. That's how Michael got that money to start that church."

I sat in awe as she spoke. I wanted to walk over to Dyson to see if he was still alive. His body had almost folded and I could no longer see his face. But Lady's eyes dared me as she kept talking.

"That damn Preston was never one to take someone being able to one up him so his hatred for Michael probably festered until Michael took his last breath. Word on the street is that Preston gone use that church to wash all his dirty money." She laughed wildly at the thought. "Preston probably assumes it's over and he'll continue his reign over St. Louis but I'm going to bring his ass to his knees and take this shit over for myself. I've had a vendetta against that man for thirty-three years. That's what this shit is about. Kill everybody…no witnesses, baby. Ain't that right Malia?"

"Yep," Malia responded with a grin.

"You snake ass bitch," I spewed at her.

"See, there she is. That's who the fuck I made. That anger that's pumpin' inside of you, I molded that shit. Through the years I fed you poison about that no good ass Michael. I nurtured that shit until you were ready to pop because I knew that pop would bring me a lot of money," she said while smiling proudly.

I couldn't believe that I had never noticed how sick and twisted she was. I knew Lady loved money but I never thought so much that she would basically make me her slave while she sat back and collected.

"I fucking hate you," I said through clenched teeth.

"I'll take it. Hate is a hell of a lot stronger emotion than love. Hate will sit and fester as you watch your best friend marry the love of yo' life. Hate will get you through lonely ass nights when your man gets up and goes home to the family he should have had with you. Hate will tell a young child that they love them because they know that child ain't never had none of it, and just like a fuckin' mut on the street, she'll be loyal to you forever."

As bad as I didn't want to cry I couldn't stop the tears from falling. I was so pissed that because of my parent's mistakes, I had inadvertently been raised by a love sick lunatic. All of this time I thought that Lady genuinely loved me.

"You claim you don't want to love but all of this shit is because you fell in love with men who belonged to someone else. You call me asshole backwards but it looks like you the one who desperately want to be loved. You're fucking desperate and pathetic, Lady."

"You gone have to fuck me harder if you want me to holler, Mykah. That weak garbage you spitting ain't stinkin' over here."

She pulled a finger nail file from her pocket and began to file her nails. Lady wasn't fazed by much. The only thing that I could do to hurt her was physically kill her because I knew she wasn't about to let me walk out alive.

"So now what? You fucked up my life, took my family from me and stole my money. Now what are you gonna do?"

"Well for starters, I'm going to keep trainin' lil Malia here. She's a quick study kind of like you but her hands ain't steady enough yet. She wanted to cash in on that bounty I put out on you. But hell, she had plenty of chances to gun your ass down but she couldn't pull through. She followed you for weeks and you didn't even know.

"Malia, was the one in the Benz?"

"Now your brain is working," Lady spat. "Rented that thing for top dollar. But she couldn't hit you, and she couldn't even kill Dyson tonight. Just wounded him. God bless her lil soul. I sure wish she had that immediate killer instinct like you 'cause when she get that quality, she should be a mighty expensive cash cow. With that high ass and killer smile, she should do two times what you done in a year or so," Lady added.

"She'll never be me, we both know that. You'll have to do that shit over my dead body."

"That's just what I intend to do. I'm gone let Malia have the pleasure of takin' out Dyson and then you'll shoot yourself. All is well that ends well, my dear."

Lady nodded her head at Malia who walked over to Dyson and shot him in his back. For the second time that night I felt bile rise up in my throat. I sobbed uncontrollably and shook my head as I watched this madness play out. Dyson's body jerked and he took a long sigh.

"This shit is crazy, Lady!" I yelled.

"That's it?" Malia questioned. " I'm kind of disappointed. I wanted my first killing to be a little more exciting. Hell, his ass was already on the brink of fucking death," Malia said with a frown on her face.

I stopped crying and had to laugh at how childish and ridiculous she sounded. Lady wanted her to take my place but the reality of the situation was that Malia was still just a little girl. She didn't have the mental capacity it took to be a killer. She was too flashy, reckless and she had the kind of mouth that would make Lady beat her upside her head at least once a day.

"You and that damn mouth of yours, get the fuck out of here. Go sit yo' ass down in the other room. I'll handle business my damn self. Damn, Mykah, you didn't teach this girl shit about followin' directions," Lady spewed at the both of us angrily.

Malia stumped out of the room with her arms crossed. She gave me the evil eye as she playfully held her finger around the trigger. I took a moment to look deeply into her eyes as she exited the room. Strangely, I still loved my child.

"You know, Mykah, I really didn't want to kill you. I was going to get that money and then ride off in the sunset so you could live the broke ass life you were going to before I raised you in the good life. Sure Malia knew what was going on with you but the rest of your family had no clue what you were up to. All you had to do was finally be a mama and that girl would have forgotten about all the times you weren't there."

"I don't need one of your fucking lectures. If you gone kill me then get the shit over with!" I yelled.

"Oh, it's coming. I was just sittin' here waitin' on my feet to calm down some. I figure you ain't got shit else to do before death so I may as well allow you to keep me company," she said with a chuckle.

"Lady, if you ever loved me, let Malia have a normal life. She's not like me. She's fragile and sensitive on the inside. She won't be able to stomach all this death. It's new to her now, but I give it a month or so and she'll be running for the hills."

"You think I don't know that. I've watched that child since birth just like you if not more than you. She spoiled and selfish but if I only get a month out of her, I'm going to book her ass up for almost every day. If she running off because this shit made her lose her mind, I ain't got nothing to do with that. I don't expect no less because she made up of weak shit just like you and yo' mama. I don't give a fuck about her just like I don't give a fuck about you."

A loud noise rang across the room and Lady slumped out of her chair. She hit the floor with a loud thud. There was a bullet in the back of her head. I looked up at the door and saw Malia standing there. She had tears running down her face and the gun was still pointed in the air. She took the gun and hit the side of her face with it over and over. Her lips and nose were both busted. I stepped back a few steps out of her eye sight. She was in some sort of psychotic trance and I hoped she would either knock herself out or forget all together that I was in the room. Her loud shrieking laughter scared me more than watching her beat her own face in.

"Don't be afraid, Mykah. After all, you did this to me. I watched you shoot Dyson and Lady and then you beat me with the gun at least that's what I'll tell the police," she said to me.

"Malia, we can leave. You don't have to call the police. We can get out of here and just run with the money. I hope you have that and not Lady," I tried to reason with her.

"My money is fine, I know exactly where it is. As for calling the police, it's too late. I did that when Lady made me sit in the other room. I was over this bullshit ass argument you two were having. I had no intentions on killing Lady, but if she handled you like that, I knew she would do me the same way. Guess I'm not as fragile and sensitive as you both thought."

I could hear the sirens clearly as they pulled in front of the house. I couldn't believe that we had all been outsmarted by a kid; my daughter at that. I shook my head as I heard the police storm the house. Malia quickly put the gun down and kicked it towards me.

"Help, help we're back here!" she screamed hysterically.

Malia ran away from the doorway just as the police forced their way into the room. I was immediately tackled to the ground. I laid there with my hands cuffed behind my back reflecting on how I'd lost everything. I looked at Lady lying there in all her black and shook my head. It was funny how her memorial service was earlier but now she was actually dead for real. It didn't have to end like that. They forced me off the ground and we were walking out of the house when I heard a paramedic scream out.

"We have a pulse, it's weak but he's alive!"

I smiled while getting in the back of the police car. I was confident that Lady was wrong about love and that Dyson's love for me had willed his heart to not give up.

Epilogue

"Mail call!" the CO yelled out disturbing me from my daily push-ups.

My arms had gotten a lot bigger than they used to be. My body was still in good shape because it was nothing to do in my cell all day other than read, talk to myself, or workout. I even paid another inmate to braid my now long ass hair going towards the back.

I looked sort of on the butch side. That was a gift and a curse in a jail full of horny women. I spent time beating ass for women approaching me sexually and was also given just about anything I wanted because they feared me.

It had been thirteen months since I'd gotten arrested. Each week I waited for my name to be called during mail drop even though I never received any. I didn't have anyone left out there for me.

My trial had been a lonely one. I was initially charged with two counts of murder and two counts of attempted murder, but when Dyson woke up from being in a coma, he confirmed what I'd been telling the police all along. Malia was the one who'd shot him and Lady.

Unfortunately for me, they let her ride off to who knows where with my money. She was so low under the radar that even the LaRues couldn't find her. Because Dyson confirmed what I said, I was only charged with Jasmine's death and the attempted murder of Jamison. I was amazed that he survived all he been through as well.

My lawyer, who was paid for by Dyson, claimed that I'd temporarily snapped when I saw my husband with another woman. A crime of passion was what they called it.

I was only charged with 2nd degree murder and was given a fifteen-year sentence. It sure as hell beat getting life, or the death penalty. For a moment the possibility of me getting the death penalty was real. Malia had forwarded the police Jamison's book and all of his research he was working on about the death of the men I had killed. The prosecution tried to pend those charges on me as well but without rock hard evidence; my defense attorney argued that the unfinished book was nothing more than Jamison's wild imagination.

It was funny seeing Preston LaRue in the courtroom the day of my sentencing. He was there in support for Dyson who was too weak to come himself. He spoke with me briefly while I was waiting in the holding cell to be transported back to the justice center. He'd forgiven Dyson but it would take more for him to even attempt to trust me. He told me he would be working on seeing if he could pull some strings and get my sentence lighter if I agreed to work for him when I got out.

In return for hiring the lawyer for me, I signed over Michael's church that he had left to me in his will to Preston. It was a peace offering on my behalf. Preston still held a lot of weight with people, even those behind bars and I knew it would be nothing for him to have me killed if he wanted to.

I was confident that as long as I stayed on the good side of the LaRues, I would be walking out of this place sometime soon. I knew it would be a bittersweet moment because I would not have Jasmine waiting for me on the other side. Out of all the things I'd gone through, I regretted her death the most. Losing her life was not worth all of the money I'd made. It was something that would haunt me for the rest of my life.

"Mykah Rice!" the CO screamed loudly.

I thought I had heard him incorrectly so I didn't move. He said my name again but with a lot of force and annoyance. I walked out slowly and looked at all the other inmates who were eagerly surrounding him waiting for their name. These people were pathetic to me. Most of them were junkies, lunatics, child abusers or dumb ass women who were taking a case for some man. I didn't fit in with any of them but they still gave me mad respect because a few of them had heard about the work I put in for Lady.

I grabbed the letter and looked in bewilderment at Lucille Rice's name in the top corner. I didn't know what the hell she could have wanted. I opened it slowly thinking that maybe Jamison had passed away or something.

Dear Mykah,

I hope this letter finds you in perfect peace. It's funny how a year ago I would have never thought I would feel it in my heart to reach out to you. It's no secret that you haven't been one of my favorite people in the world. I say all that to say, I forgive you. It is by the grace of God that I'm able to say that. I never thought that I would get to a spot in my life where I am no longer drinking and living my life for someone other than Jamison. Finding the Lord was one of the best decisions I ever made. I never knew a love like this. It really is an experience that I wish you do find the time to have. I must admit that when I woke this morning, I didn't have any intentions on writing you. I'd pushed you to the back of my mind as I began my journey with God, but as soon as I got off my knees, I walked straight to the table and started writing you. That's the good thing about accepting Jesus in your life. Everyone talks about wanting a relationship that's fresh and spontaneous, I get all of that from Him and I dare you to try Him! I wish I had a long time ago and then you and I would have had a better relationship. Maybe I could have saved you all from this attack by the devil. I won't harp on the past though. I only want to walk in faith in the future. I won't hold you much longer I just wanted to let you know that even in your darkest hour, you have a friend in Jesus. Take care of yourself in there.

Faithfully speaking, *Lucille*

P.S. Jamison has been making a lot of progress. He was able to move his fingers this week so the doctors are really expecting him to gain use of his arm again. They're really taking good care of him in the rehab facility.

Hopefully I'll be able to bring him home soon. He's going to get a big kick out of me reaching out to you but I'm sure it will make him happy deep down. He really loved you. Maybe you should write him sometime.

Take care!

I sat the letter down and wiped the tears from my eyes. The more I wiped them away, the more they fell. I just gave up the fight of trying to hide them. I didn't care who walked by and saw me. Receiving a letter from Lucille with news about Jamison was something I wanted to celebrate.

I had cried for so long for my situation that crying happy tears actually felt like a weight had been lifted from my shoulder. The fact that Jamison was making progress filled me with newfound hope. It made me question if I wanted to continue with my plan to unite with the LaRues or maybe Lucille was right and God really did produce miracles.

If He could change her then I knew anything would be possible for me.

Also by Chris Renee

Wealthy & WICKED

A Novel By
CHRIS RENEE

For More Book Titles Please Visit

www.lifechangingbooks.net

facebook.com/lifechangingbooks
Twitter: @lcbooks
Instagram:@lcbbooks

Dirty Divorce pt 1
Dirty Divorce pt 2
Dirty Divorce pt 3
Dirty Divorce pt 4
Welfare Grind
Still Grindin'
Welfare Grind pt 3
Game Over
Married to a Balla
Life After a Balla
Gangsta Bitch
Love Heist
Paparazzi
V.I.P
Left For Dead
Good Girl Gone
Bad
Woman Scorned
Next Door Nympho

Chedda Boyz
Bruised
Bruised pt 2
One Night Stand
Another One
Night Stand
Wealthy and
Wicked
Cashin' Out
Bedroom Gangsta
Daddy's House
Expensive Taste
Millionaire Mistress pt 1
Still a Mistress
Millionaire Mistress pt 3
Naughty Lil Angel
Mistress Loose
Tricked
Charm City

231

CHECK OUT THESE LCB SEQUELS

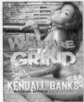

LCB BOOK TITLES

See More Titles At
www.lifechangingbooks.net

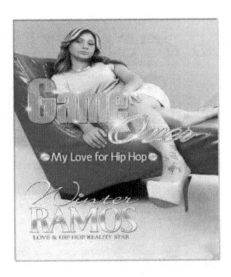

Winter Ramos, one of the new faces of VH1's hit reality television show, Love and Hip Hop New York Season 3 delivers a brazen and unabashed memoir of her life in the world of hip hop. In Game Over, Winter puts all of her emotions on the page leaving no experience, emotional abuse, or former lover uncovered. From her days as assistant to rapper, Fabolous and friend to Jada Kiss, to appearing on Love and Hip Hop and being Creative Costume Designer for Flavor unit Films, Winter delivers a tell-all book on her famous ex-lovers and experiences in the music industry. As the chick that was always in the mix and cool with everyone, Winter was privy to the cray beyond the videos, private flights, and limos that the cameras caught for us. Her reality and theirs was no game. Game Over is Winter's cautionary tale for the next generation of young women who believe that the fabulous lives of celebrities unveiled in blogs and on reality television shows are all FIRE! Stay tuned, because this GAME is about to get real.

In Stores Now!!!

CPSIA information can be obtained at www.ICGtesting.com
Printed in the USA
LVOW01s2142200614

391085LV00011B/138/P